A Generous Spirit

Inanna Pubications gratefully acknowledges the support of the Canada Council
for the Arts and the Ontario Arts Council for our publishing program. We also
acknowledge the financial support of the Government of Canada.

Design: Nieves Guerra.
Transcription: Talia Sieff   Copyedit: Christina Graben.
Cover photo: Beth Brant, photographed by Tee Corinne. From Tee A. Corinne
Papers, Coll 263, Special Collections & University Archives, University of
Oregon, Eugene, Or. Used with permission.

Library and Archives Canada Cataloguing in Publication

Title: A generous spirit : selected work by Beth Brant / edited by Janice Gould.
Other titles: Works. Selections
Names: Brant, Beth, 1941-2015, author. I Gould, Janice, 1949-2019, editor.
Series: Sapphic classics. I Inanna poetry & fiction series.
Description: Series statement: Sapphic classics I Inanna poetry and fiction series I
Identifiers: Canadiana (print) 20190147652 I Canadiana (ebook) 20190147679
I ISBN 9781771336857 (softcover) I ISBN 9781771336864 (epub) I ISBN
9781771336871 (Kindle) I ISBN 9781771336888 (pdf)
Classification: LCC PS8553.R2958 A6 2019 I DDC C813/.54—dc23

Printed and bound in USA

Sinister Wisdom, Inc.
2333 McIntosh Road
Dover, FL 33527
sinisterwisdom@gmail.com
www.sinisterwisdom.org

Inanna Publications and Education Inc.
210 Founders College, York University
4700 Keele Street, Toronto, Ontario, Canada M3J 1P3
Telephone: (416) 736-5356 Fax: (416) 736-5765
Email: inanna.publications@inanna.ca Website: www.inanna.ca

A Generous Spirit

Selected Work by Beth Brant

Edited by
Janice Gould

Foreword by
Lee Maracle

Afterword by
Deborah Miranda

sapphic classics from
SINISTER WISDOM

inanna poetry & fiction series

INANNA PUBLICATIONS & EDUCATION INC.
TORONTO, CANADA

Contents

Foreword

So few Indigenous women were publishing in 1981 when Beth Brant came forward with her first work. In those days, the few of us that were writing were so hungry for each other's work that we snapped her up. She transformed us. Some of us knew about lesbians and homosexuals, transgendered and fluid gendered people in our communities before Europeans came and transformed us, but we were quiet about it. All of us have relatives who are two-spirited, but Beth jumped into the fray, courageous, and became the first Indigenous lesbian writer from Canada. It–she–changed my life.

No matter it comes from oppression, the absence of freedom, curtailing and prohibiting the right to love, is a sickness. Beth talked about that with all of us in those days; we were so few we clung together and cherished one another. No one was trying to pull the other down. We all sought to hold each other up. Moreover, Beth was best at it. We went to the International Feminist Book Fair in Montreal together, and to the next one in Europe together. In addition, we heard each other's stories.

Her life was too short, like so many of our people. Colonial poverty and oppression took away some of our best sons and daughters. Beth left early, but she had accomplished so much. She inspired a generation of two-spirited authors who followed her to publication. There would be not have been a *Johnny Appleseed* without there first being a Beth Brant. There would have been no Connie Fife without Beth Brant. There would be no *I Am Woman* without Beth Brant. We were feminists when everyone objected. Feminism is a white thing, they said. Beth's response, so is patriarchy, and then she told us about the friendship between Elizabeth Cady Stanton and an Iroquoian woman that sparked the suffragettes–made sense to me.

Homophobia and sexism are two sides to the same patriarchal oppressive coin. Beth made that clear to all of us. Few people know that her introduction to one of her books launched another aspect to our wellness movement: heal the healers? In a conversation with Aiyana Maracle, Beth asked her: But who will heal the healers?

Aiyanna had not transitioned at the time, but became close to Beth, and I recall overhearing their conversations. It was a privilege to listen. Beth had an understanding of the road to freedom, the path to love, and the story we would have to create to get there. The pearls in her stories lie in a shell of words that need only to be opened; read Beth's work and we can all come together, transgendered, heterosexual, homosexual, lesbian, fluid gendered, disabled, and abled, white, and non-white. We do not have to be stuck where corporate colonialism consigned us. There was room for everyone in Beth's heart. We can reach out and resist. The world is ours; we just need to go get it. This was Beth's philosophy.

This book is special. It marks the beginning of the Indigenous publishing movement. Everyone should read it.

Lee Maracle
July 2019

Working Class Dreams:
An Introduction to the Work
of Beth Brant

Bay of Quinte Mohawk writer Beth Brant (Degonwadonti) was born in her grandparents' house in Detroit, Michigan, in the year 1941. Her parents were Joseph Brant (Mohawk) and Hazel Brant (Scots-Irish). Pregnant at seventeen, Beth Brant married when she was eighteen and, in the ensuing years, had three daughters. In 1973, after fourteen years of marriage, she divorced and became a single mom, settling in Melvindale, Michigan, a suburb of Detroit, where she supported herself and her children through a variety of odd jobs—waitress, salesclerk, cleaning woman. Beth acknowledged that she had felt an attraction to her close girlfriends when she was teenager. Later, as various liberation movements flowered in the 1960s and 70s, she claimed her lesbian identity. In 1976 or '77 she became partners with Denise Dorsz, the co-founder of a feminist coffee house in Detroit that opened in 1971, Poor Woman's Paradise.[1] They were partners for over twenty years.

Beth began writing in 1981, at the age of forty, and she considered her words a gift from the spirit world. The small outpouring of her work includes essays, short stories, and poetry. At the urging of Adrienne Rich and Michelle Cliff, who were co-editing the lesbian art and literature journal *Sinister Wisdom* at the time, Beth served

---

1 Denise Dorsz is profiled in the book, *Finding the Movement: Sexuality, Contested Space, and Feminist Activism*, by Anne/Finn Enke. The publisher's note explains, "In *Finding the Movement*, Enke reveals that diverse women's engagement with public spaces gave rise to and profoundly shaped second-wave feminism. Focusing on women's activism in Detroit, Chicago, and Minneapolis-St. Paul during the 1960s and 1970s, Enke describes how women across race and class created a massive groundswell of feminist activism by directly intervening in the urban landscape."

Dorsz is now the Executive Director of Leaps and Bounds Family Services, a non-profit agency that offers education programs and services to families and children.

http://www.leapsnbounds.org/home_112015.aspx

as the guest editor of a volume of Native American women's writing: *A Gathering of Spirit*, published by *Sinister Wisdom* (1983) and later reissued by Nancy Bereano's Firebrand Books (1988). This volume for *Sinister Wisdom* emerged from a conversation Beth had with Michelle and Adrienne when they were living in Massachusetts. On a snowy evening in January 1982, Beth, as a guest at their house, asked Michelle and Adrienne if they had ever considered devoting an issue of *Sinister Wisdom* to Native women's writing. When they suggested that she could edit such a collection, Beth was taken aback, worrying that she would not be up for the task, lacking, as she did, a high school diploma, let alone a college degree. Yet through this work and her further writing, Beth developed a passionate voice. She became well-known among Native American and First Nations writers, other women of color writers and poets, many of whom were lesbian, and the world at large.

Sinister Wisdom 22/23: *A Gathering of Spirit* was not the first anthology of contemporary Native American writing to be published in the United States. A decade earlier saw the publication of *The Man to Send Rain Clouds: Contemporary Stories by American Indians* (1974), edited by Kenneth Rosen and featuring writers like Leslie Silko, Simon Ortiz, Anna Lee Walters, and other Indian writers who were primarily associated with the Southwest, with the University of New Mexico, or with the Santa Fe Indian School and the Institute of American Indian Art (IAIA) in Santa Fe. A year later, Rosen's *Voices of the Rainbow: Contemporary Poetry by Native Americans*, included Silko and Walters, as well as poets Gerald Vizenor, Carter Revard, Anita Endrezze (Probst), Ray Young Bear, and others. In 1979, the University of New Mexico Press published *The Remembered Earth: An Anthology of Native American Literature*, a more comprehensive volume of writing edited by Geary Hobson. Perhaps the most prominent among these contemporary voices was N. Scott Momaday, whose novel *House Made of Dawn* won a Pulitzer Prize in 1969, and ushered in a renewed interest in American Indian writing among non-Native academics and others. Many of the writers involved with these works had already published stellar volumes of poetry, short stories, and novels—or would go on to do so in the next few years. These and other books by American Indian writers helped set the stage for the writing that appeared in *A Gathering of Spirit* and Beth's other works.[2]

However, it was not Native American publishing alone that helped to create a place for Beth's writing to appear. A nexus of social changes (including American Indian activism), a revisionist impulse in the writing of American history vis-à-vis American Indians, and the emergence of Ethnic Studies and Native American Studies, specifically at the university level, helped augment public interest in Indigenous American writing. The inclusion of American Indian literature in some English departments and women's studies programs also served to make a space for Native writers, some of whom, like Silko, Welch, Harjo, Momaday, and Vizenor, eventually became canonical.

Neither American Indian writing in the 1970s nor the writing that came into flower in the 1980s—much of which was produced by women—would have found as wide an audience without the development in the 1970s of small presses. These presses offered a voice and support to women writers (including white lesbians, lesbians of color, and working class Gay and straight women) and facilitated the rise of independent women's publishing enterprises and bookstores. From Shameless Hussy Press,[3] founded in 1969 and billed as the first feminist press in the United States, to the Women's Press Collective in Oakland, California, to a plethora of

---

2 *That's What She Said: Contemporary Poetry and Fiction by Native American Women*, edited by Rayna Greene, was published in 1984, but as far as I know, no "out" lesbian writers were included in that volume.

3 The Library at the University of California, Santa Cruz, notes the following: "One of the most important historical contributions of Shameless Hussy Press was the first publication of books by four women who later become prominent feminist writers: Pat Parker, Mitsuye Yamada, Ntozake Shange, and Susan Griffin." Shameless Hussy was founded by Alta (Alta Gerrey). An archive of her recollections may be viewed at https://library.ucsc.edu/reg-hist/alta. Readers may also wish to obtain *The Complete Works of Pat Parker (Sinister Wisdom 102)*, with an Introduction by Judy Grahn, and edited by Julie Enszer, part of the Sapphic Classic series.

other women's, lesbian, working class, people of color, and left-wing publishing venues, an explosion of printed matter became available. One aim of this grass roots publishing was to "raise consciousness," as it was termed, and provide information on social justice issues, including women's access to health and education, and the question of female exclusion from positions of political power and authority. Much of the collective activity and writing that began to emerge from this ferment was consciously anti-racist and anti-homophobic.[4] It questioned and challenged the multiple social oppressions operating through a corporate-capitalist-colonialist, patriarchal system that virtually ensured women's erasure and could violently coerce women's silence. A significant part of this discourse was coming from women of color, whether lesbian or straight.

When *This Bridge Called My Back: Writings by Radical Women of Color,* edited by Cherríe Moraga and Gloria Anzaldúa, erupted in feminist circles in 1981, it became a primary text for feminist writers and thinkers of color. I would guess that a space opened up for Beth that allowed her to imagine "weaving together" a volume of writing that she believed was "urgent." It would be comprised of "physical details...spiritual labor...ritual...gathering... [and] making" (8). She saw her editing as an "unraveling" of the cloth that brought these American Indian women writers together, but also as a weaving that could stitch the threads, "each one with its distinct color and texture," into a new cloth made of this spirit-gathering. In this sense, it parallels the vision of *This Bridge* that was a platform for a sisterhood comprised of "Sisters of the yam Sisters of the rice Sisters of the corn Sisters of the plantain," as Toni Cade Bambara explains in the Foreword to that volume's First Edition (xxix). But Beth's perception of her work, as she conceived of it in her Introduction, was quieter and less consciously a call to action

---

4 For an excellent discussion of the crucial role feminist bookstores played in making women's writing available, and in promoting antiracist discourse and analysis among lesbian feminists, see *The Feminist Bookstore Movement: Lesbian Antiracism and Feminist Accountability,* by Kristen Hogan.

(though no less radical) than Bambara's serious-playful dialoguing. In her Introduction, Beth's syntax is precise, and for a woman who called herself "uneducated," this seems a pointed and important decision.[5] Beth was aware of how crucial the job was of selecting and arranging the work submitted for *A Gathering of Spirit*, as well as the way she created a context for understanding and appreciating it. She wanted to do justice to the work she had gathered, to clarify its significance—and just as critically, to show the ritual of its inception and birth, to highlight its strength and beauty, to make a space for the anger, despair, and desperation that she opened herself to by editing this volume. She understood that part of her task was to connect with the writers who sent her their work—along with their queries and questions that were not always about writing—and to connect those writers together. *A Gathering of Spirit* is a unique creation in many ways. Beth wanted to include the voices that would not ordinarily be heard, that would not typically find a place in American letters—those voices of prison inmates, of women living on reservations or in Indian enclaves in big cities, the voices of single, sometimes lesbian mothers, of women who engaged in physical labor to make a living and support a family.

While Beth selected writing by Indian women who were to become or were already a part of the academic world, she was democratic and non-canonical in her choices for *A Gathering of Spirit*. Just as important to the volume is the imaginative work, and "erotics," of gay Native women. As literary critic Lisa Tatonetti points out in her essay, "The Emergence and Importance of Queer American Indian Literatures...," Beth's anthology is "[n]otable on a number of levels, [it being] the first collection of American Indian writing to be edited exclusively by an American Indian. In addition, its importance to the development of queer Native literature cannot be overrated as the anthology includes pieces

---

5 Despite Beth's admission about dropping out of school, she was apparently an autodidact. According to Denise Dorsz, "Both Beth and her father were voracious readers" (e-mail correspondence, September 1, 2018).

by eleven Native lesbians...." (148). The inclusion of lesbian Native voices, including Beth's own, broke with a tradition of erasure of Two-Spirit identity, which had been excluded in the emerged and emerging canon of American Indian literature. The "silences and omissions" among literary critics in the field of American Indian literary arts, which Tatonetti insightfully explores in her essay, also contributed to the sense that "lit-crit" gate-keepers (no doubt some of them Native American) were busily deciding whose work was worthy of admission and discussion—and it was not that of "out" American Indian lesbians.[6]

A Gathering of Spirit might not have had immediate critical success in the larger world were it not for Nancy Bereano, who believed in the work and kept it in print through her press, Firebrand Books. This dedication shows that Beth's selection of writers proved compelling to some readers. It is not simply Beth's inclusiveness that likely interests readers, but the ways in which she constructs a Native identity through her accessible language of caring and compassion. It may strike some readers as odd that Beth's Two-Spirit-ness is centered as much on care as on sexuality, yet friendship is an important attribute in lesbian relationships.

Beth and I probably corresponded before we met in person, and we became good friends when she traveled to the West Coast to do readings. I remember sitting with her in the dining room of my old Berkeley house, where I lived with my parents, my older sister, and her little son. It may have been around 1983. Mom sat with us that afternoon, as we talked and laughed over cups of coffee. Beth had been awarded a writing residency on the Marin Headlands, and was a bit apprehensive about going there. I had agreed to drive her out to the residency, since I knew many of the back roads in the area, and I looked forward to showing Beth a part of the California coast that I loved.

---

6 The term Two-Spirit was not available to Beth when she put together her anthology, but it became current around 1990 when a number of LGBTQ Indians gathered at a conference in Winnipeg, Saskatchewan. Tatonetti reminds readers that as early as 1968, Sue-Ellen Jacobs had explored the existence of gender-variant biologically male individuals, typically called "berdache," the term formerly assigned to male Two-Spirit people in anthropological literature and now thought of as a derogatory term.

Beth and I continued to correspond after she went back to Michigan. I remember recording music for her, making her a tape of some of the accordion tunes I played, and perhaps some of the old songs I enjoyed singing during that time, like "Leatherwing Bat" and "Which Side Are You On?" Although I had been published in small press publications before, I was grateful to have a few poems included in *A Gathering of Spirit*. I have Beth to thank, too, because she took the initiative to send a manuscript of my poems to Nancy Bereano, urging her to consider publishing them. In 1990, Firebrand published my first book of poetry, *Beneath My Heart*.

Beth's generosity and warmth can also be seen in her correspondence with Raven, an incarcerated woman of Eastern Cherokee heritage, who was on death row in a Maryland prison. While Raven tells Beth, "I'm not into women, or at least, I haven't been..." (225), their letters to one another are warm with a kind of familiarity that marks them not merely in "sisterhood," but as "relatives" or "relations." This becomes painfully clear when Beth explains why "choosing life over death" is important. Such a statement to a woman potentially facing the gas chamber did not come out of callousness on Beth's part, but I think was meant to "give heart" to Raven, to not allow herself to die inwardly, metaphorically, from discouragement and despair, or from cynicism.[7] Accompanying Beth's letter to Raven is a copy of *This Bridge Called My Back*, which Beth declares is "a book that made a great change in my life" (223). She continues with this confession:

> What I want to say is that I'm frightened much of the time. I may never know what it is like to be in prison. But I have been in a mental institution, unable to get out, unable to go to the bathroom with asking. Unable to stop the harassment by the nurses, by the orderlies. Unable to stop the drugs they shoved down my throat. When I refused to

---

7   "In 1982, Doris Ann Foster ["Raven"] was convicted of fatally stabbing a hotel owner Josephine Dietrich, 71, with a screwdriver during a robbery at a North East motel. Two juries convicted her. Five years later, then-Gov. Harry Hughes granted Foster clemency on his last day in office, reducing her capital sentence to life without parole," http://www.baltimoresun.com/bal-md.penalty21oct21-story.html.

eat, they stuck needles in me to feed me. They threatened me with shock treatments, with insulin therapy. There was a point where I had to decide to live or to die. I chose life for myself. At that point I didn't know why I did. But now I know I am needed for something. I would never have known you. And I am blessed by knowing you...(224).

Whether Beth believes in Raven's innocence or not, she does not say. Her task in writing to Raven, it seems, is to be an ambassador of trust, to inspire the intimacy of trust through the revelation of a personal story, to establish a relationship through a kind of affinity borne of disclosure. What Beth seems to be saying to Raven is, "We need your story; we need to learn from your story." And what we need to learn is what it means to survive—mentally, physically, and spiritually—under conditions often unfairly imposed, thrust upon us by the circumstances of our gender, our sexual preference, our language, status, place of our birth, color of our skin. But we need also to learn compassion, or as some would say, the empathy that comes from being able, and even daring ourselves, to imagine another's life with its pain, joy, suffering, or celebration.

The themes of survival and empathy permeate Beth's entire oeuvre, whether she is speaking in her own voice or creating the timbre of a character's voice, someone whose story has not been told in a place where it could be heard, where it would be audible. As Beth develops as a writer, she increases the range of voices available to her ear. She is most interested in vernacular speech, and even in her early work, the stories and recollections in *Mohawk Trail*, she is adept at creating convincing characters with distinct dialects, whether in first- or third-person narrations. Thus, storytelling, which emerges from Native oral traditions, and continuance, which surfaces from the need to survive in a sustainable way, are themes that are woven into Beth's literary offerings. These themes seem to be a feature of twentieth-century writing, and they have been taken up by American Indian/First Nations people, and by other people of color, for a very long time, if colonial court records are any indication. In the world of literature that Beth may have been familiar with, a voice like Audre Lorde's could have provided the kind of emotional sustenance to be a writer and to do the writing. In her 1978 poem, "A Litany for Survival," for example, Lorde writes,

> when our stomachs are empty we are afraid
> we may never eat again
> when we are loved we are afraid
> love will vanish
> when we are alone we are afraid
> love will never return
> and when we speak we are afraid
> our words will not be heard
> nor welcomed
> but when we are silent
> we are still afraid
>
> So it is better to speak
> remembering
> we were never meant to survive.[8]

Beth was deeply and obviously in tune with the stories of survival against the odds, her sense that "we were never meant to survive," and she confides in her letter to Raven, quoted above, "I have spent too long hating myself, and I don't want to anymore" (223). She further discloses, "My lover is white. She comes from a poor Polish family. She understands so well [self-hatred]. Probably because she was raised so poor. She knows what it is like to be despised and to be ashamed" (223). There is a reckoning here as Beth articulates the mutual oppressions she shares with her woman lover, especially the understanding that comes from knowing what it means to be "despised" and "ashamed." Dealing with these

---

8 "A Litany for Survival." Copyright 1978 by Audre Lorde, from *The Collected Poems of Audre Lorde*, https://www.poetryfoundation.org/poems/147275/a-litany-for-survival.

powerful feelings becomes part of the impetus to write, fuel for dispelling the damage inflicted, a way of defusing the potent harm that can be triggered over and over through the injustice of racism, sexism, classism, and homophobia.

Beth recognized all these "objective" categories of oppression that, over time, we internalize, adopting the scorn and disgust we experience outwardly and turning it in on ourselves. Her editorial work and her writing, whether in poems, stories, or essays, were attempts to come to terms—and shape a language—that speaks the truth of love and desire, hope and passion, and faith in the goodness of friendship, family, and the natural world, especially in the face of private turmoil, self-doubt, shame, and self-loathing. What a gift for us that Beth had the means and ability to craft and share what she did in a relatively short writing life of thirty or so years.

The themes of survival, empathy, storytelling, and continuance parallel Beth's use of "the Physical...the Spiritual...the Ritual... [and] the Gathering" in her Introduction to *Mohawk Trail*. Her list concludes with "the Making," so, to complete the parallel, we might submit the word "transformation" to the themes listed above. In many of her stories, Beth is interested in how or why a character transforms. In "Coyote Learns a New Trick," for example, Coyote decides to play a trick on Fox, "that la-di-da female who was forever grooming her pelt and telling stories about how clever and sly she was" (*Mohawk Trail*, 32). The story itself is something of a transformation, since Beth's Coyote is not the typical male character of traditional tales who is forever causing trouble for himself or others, but is instead a mother coyote with pups. True to Coyote character, however, Beth creates a trickster who, in this story, decides to cross-dress to see if she can successfully make a fool of Fox. The transformation is achieved when, after piecing together a complete outfit of men's attire, Coyote looks in the mirror and "almost die[s] laughing. She look[s] like a very dapper male of style" (32). She struts off to Fox's den.

All kinds of "reclamations" as well as transformations are going on in this story. Beth's Coyote finds herself in the cheerful company of a very wily Fox, a classic "femme" straight out of the "butch/ femme" tradition. There seems to be evidence that the use of the terms "butch" and "femme" were out of vogue in the 1970s and 1980s as middle class feminists developed discourse on the negative effects of the patriarchy.[9]

If this is the case, then Beth's employing and playing with the dichotomy could be a kind of working-class reclamation of the images, if not the terms, of butch and femme. When creatures in Coyote's social world, represented by Hawk and Turtle, either deride her or consider her "weird," Coyote is at first nonchalant, saying to herself, "....hawks have been known to have no sense of humor," but later, after Turtle scuttles away, Coyote begins to feel that her "plan was not going so well" (32). She persists nevertheless, because she believes she can pull a fast one on Fox. Her coyote inclinations to disrupt the social world, even if it brings her a bit of dismay, are strong enough to override the reactions she gets.

Beth is presenting a character from Native oral traditions who at once fits right in to the tradition (Coyote is known to cross-dress, disguising himself as a woman in order to have access to females) and at the same time is disobedient to the tradition since Brant's Coyote seems to be innocent of her own butch-lesbian inclinations, even as she plays them out. While in a traditional Coyote story, Coyote may outsmart and seduce the women he's after, in Beth's story, Fox's sexy, femme-like antics take Coyote by surprise. She turns the trick back on Coyote, but in a good way as the two female creatures get down to the "*serious* business" of making love (34). In this way, Beth exploits the Two-Spirit potential of Coyote, and the outcome is mutually beneficial, since even if Coyote was not aware of her own desires, Fox's "gaydar" ferrets out Coyote's intentions very easily. Fox disallows Coyote's trick and, in the process, helps Coyote transform into a more "authentic" sexual self, a female person who could love (or at least enjoy love-making with) another female.

---

9 See, for example, Sara Crawley's article, "Are Butch and Fem Working-Class and Antifeminist?" in *Gender and Society*, April 2001.

The conflict of desires Beth explores in her work is often as much spiritual as it is physical. The desire for meaning and fulfillment in one's work is a common theme, but this is shown rather than told. Working class lessons are abundant in this writer's stories, from describing daily labor, to witnessing how workers are used and abused, to dealing with racism and sexism. In "Garnett Lee," the title character, a "hillbilly" from Appalachia, finds comfort in reading books after losing her factory job, a pastime her mother teases her about, but which also makes the mother proud. In "Terri," a half-Chippewa, half-Polish "go-go-dancer" achieves a sense of satisfaction by dancing for the "ladies" in a lesbian bar. She says, "I don't got any kids, but when I dance I feel like it's kinda telling a story. You know what I mean? I want the ladies who paid good money to see me to get in a mood that makes them happy. It's not just wanting to do a good job for the tips, but I want to do a good job for them" (51). There is pride of accomplishment in Terri's words, a sense of service, an acknowledgment of her value as someone who can convey a "story" that brings happiness, even briefly, to women whose lives are probably anything but easy. The "tough dykes" that populate this working class bar may brawl over an attractive woman, or they may buy her "pretty clothes" with their hard-earned dough, but they're appreciative customers, and unlike the men in straight bars, they keep their hands to themselves.

"Working class dreams!" says Danny (58), the title character of another story. The dreams are driven by the urge to get out from under "the man," from under the day-to-day grind that dehumanizes men toiling on an assembly line, and that brutalizes women serving those men, who feel it's their right to demean them, to "fuck [them] over" (57). Danny is aware that his "upwardly mobile" aspiration to be a nurse goes against the ethos of masculinity represented by his father, who "gets on [Danny's] case" and "beats the shit outta [him]" when he finds Danny dressed in women's clothing (58). Again, Brant brings sympathetic attention not just to the conditions of the laboring class, but to a young man more comfortable feeling like— and "being"—a woman. As mentioned above, this works appears some years before the term "Two-Spirit" is available, and long before many in the LGBTQ community reclaimed the word "queer" as a positive designation. In any event, Danny's ethnic heritage is Irish, but this does not immunize him from the opprobrium heaped on his family by some who call them "dirty Irish" and "shanty pigs" (58). Well aware of this ethno-centrism, the sexist attitudes directed against women, and the homophobia aimed at cross-dressers, Danny refers to himself as a "freak," and self-medicates with drugs as a way to numb himself to the pain of humiliations of his life, but also to the cruel mistreatment of children that he witnesses on his ward, little kids damaged from beatings and rapes (59).

The economy of language in these vignettes and stories is a mark of how well-crafted Beth's writing is, for she is able to convey in her tightly drawn portraits a sense of the social worlds in which her protagonists live, and the difficulties they are up against. And while some of those lives end unhappily, the struggle to assert their own humanity, their own truth, is a central motivator for Beth's characters. Metaphorically, the people Beth creates grapple with separations and alienations imposed by economic or social necessity. Frequently, they are in search of contentment, a condition that suggests a kind of fulfillment that is the result of acceptance. Whether folks are attempting to find happiness, strictly speaking, does not seem to be the point. For example, Elijah, an older Mohawk man in Beth's story "Food & Spirits," in her collection by the same name, travels by bus from the Tyendinaga Reserve to the city to visit his twin granddaughters Annie and Alice. Because the twins are delayed by an auto accident on the freeway, a fact Elijah only learns later, the old man must wait for them to show up. In the course of waiting, Elijah befriends a young black man, Terrence, who directs him to an African-American bar across the street from the bus depot, where he can await his granddaughters without being hassled by the bus station personnel. We might gather from Terrence's unstated caution that if you're black or Indian—or any person of color, for that matter—you'll be treated with suspicion by the authorities, even if you're "carefully dressed," like Elijah.

Beth uses this story as a way to explore loss, specifically the death of one's child or children, and also the passing of a spouse. Elijah has lost at least three people in his life, his wife Edie and his twin sons, who are not named in the story. While the bartender, Archibald looks on, Elijah discusses these losses with Alana, a young mixed-blood African-American who watched her one-year-old baby girl die in her arms from an undiagnosed illness. Elijah's kindness, frankness, and patient demeanor help Alana to open up about her bereavement. "Food & Spirits" is also a vehicle for talking about the fact of the spirit world, which from Elijah's point of view is a naturally occurring phenomenon. He seeks to explain this to Alana:

> Elijah looked away from the two people [Archibald and Alana]. Talking about Edie, [Alana's daughter] Cherry Marie, and his baby boys made him lonely, made him long for the sweet faces of the twin girls he loved so much. He felt a hand on his shoulder.
> 'Don't be feeling bad, Elijah,' Alana said.
> 'Oh, I ain't feelin' bad, just a little lonesome for my twins. But you know, it's good to talk about death. It's funny, we treat life like it ain't no big deal when it's the biggest deal there is. And we get scared to talk about death. It's just the everyday, death is. Here, have another piece of bread. When you bite into something like this, you know how good life is.'
> He handed a piece of [fry] bread to Alana and took one for himself (83).

Elijah's fry bread, prepared for him by his daughter-in-law before his trip, is symbolic of sharing with others the joys with which we are blessed, and the grief we must endure in life. The fry bread is special: it's Indian food, it's delicious, and through its sharing, through the communion of friendship and conversation, it feeds hungry souls.

Time and again in her stories, Beth seeks to feed her readers, providing nourishment through the power of language to connect us imaginatively with other lives, other experiences, similar to or estranged from our own. In this way, Beth was an educator, and in her life as a writer, she was provided with opportunities to travel to workshops and conferences both domestically in the U.S. and abroad. She maintained a strong connection to her Canadian relatives and friends, and by virtue of this not-formalized dual citizenship was awarded writing grants from both Canadian and

U.S. funding sources. One of her most prized experiences was a residency at Tyendinaga where she was able to interview a number of elders, resulting in the oral history titled *I'll Sing Til the Day I Die: Conversations with Tyendinaga Elders*. In this non-fiction work, she is able to bring to the page the voices of elders who recall generations of stories, the words passed down by ancestors, and their own reflections on how things used to be and how they are today. A common thread in these stories concerns the loss of the Native tongue because of the government-imposed mandate of the Residential Schools, similar to the federal boarding school system in the United States. Here is what Eve Maracle, born in 1896, had to say:

> My mother and dad spoke Mohawk. But I'll tell you something, in my generation we were not allowed to say one word of Mohawk language. And that was the government did that. So this is why we don't understand the Mohawk language, and that's a shame. Of course, they're starting to have classes, teaching the children and they have adult classes. I learned it there. The grown-ups always spoke the language to one another, and they did to us kids until we went to school, and that's what happened. And then they were afraid to talk to the children in Mohawk, for fear of what might happen. They didn't know what might happen, if maybe the kids would be taken away, or punished. That was really, really bad (19-20).

This cataclysmic disruption of family and community life through the imposition of English in the residential and boarding school era is a long-standing grief and grievance. The ways we could and should have been nourished through the mother's tongue, through our Native languages, we experience as not just a deep loss, but as a terrible wound. The multiple damages done to First Nations and Native Peoples on this Turtle Island are numerous and difficult to talk about. That is why collections like the ones Beth put together are so important—both the oral histories she collected and the short fiction she produced. Her audience was and is her immediate relatives, but the circle spirals out to the larger world, for all our relatives, including non-Indians, as well as our other-than-human relations—eagle, hawk, falcon, turtle, salmon, deer, blue heron, and others. Beth may have considered her stories a gift from the spirit world, but they were also a way for her to honor that world, to esteem the voices of people no longer with us, the voices that congregate not at the margins, but at the center of any writer's life, at the center of any existence.

Finally, a word about her non-fiction writing, in the book Beth titled *Writing as Witness: Essay and Talk*, published in 1994 by the Women's Press in Toronto. She recognized this collection as a gathering of "essay, talk, and theory," noting in her initial sentence that "words are sacred" (3). The book was completed as Beth was recovering from her second bypass surgery, meant "to correct wayward and blocked femoral arteries" (4). In her introduction to the volume she expresses her gratitude to friends and family, and notes how important is "the continuance of history, story, and the People" (4).

Continuance is a watchword. In one sense, it represents what Beth means by "theory," because it proposes the idea that despite the almost complete genocide of Indian people in this hemisphere— our near physical, emotional, and mental annihilation—something of the spirit still resides within us. It is the fuel that energizes her protagonists to fight their demons, to reclaim their histories, to express their love and desire for another, to establish their authority as elders, to offer bread to one another, to die with dignity. These are sacred acts because they are the acts that make us human, despite our flaws, our inconsistencies, our fears and vulnerabilities. But we cannot know how to be and become human without words, specifically without the words that shape our sacred continuance.

Beth saw her writing as an enacting of responsibility—the responsibility to help bring us all to the knowledge of how to live with integrity, as good human beings: in balance, centered in the heart's knowledge, hopeful, not vengeful, not small, but with generosity. Whether she achieved this in her own life to her own satisfaction, I don't know, and it is not mine to say. But in my view, that is where her writing is meant to take us: to ignite the imagination, to provide it with a kind of knowledge about how to care about those who suffer, and about how to walk in one's full posture, in a sacred way, looking at the world with vision. Beth Brant crossed over from this world on August 6, 2015.

Janice Gould
Colorado Springs, Colorado
October 2018

Works Cited

Brant, Beth. *A Gathering of Spirit*. Ithaca, NY: Firebrand Books, 1984, 1988.

Brant, Beth. *Mohawk Trail*. Ithaca, NY: Firebrand Books, 1985.

Brant, Beth. *Food & Spirits*. Ithaca, NY: Firebrand Books, 1991.

Brant, Beth. *Writing as Witness: Essay and Talk*. Toronto, Ontario, Canada: Women's Press, 1994.

Brant, Beth. *I'll Sing Til the Day I Die: Conversations with Tyendinaga Elders*. Toronto, Ontario, Canada: Women's Press, 1995.

Lorde, Audre. "A Litany for Survival." https://www.poetryfoundation. org/poems/147275/a-litany-for-survival.

Moraga, Cherríe and Gloria Anzaldúa, editors. *This Bridge Called My Back: Writings by Radical Women of Color*, 4th edition. Albany, NY: SUNY Press, 2015.

Tatonetti, Lisa. "The Emergence and Importance of Queer American Indian Literatures: or, "Help and Stories" in Thirty Years of SAIL." *Studies in American Indian Literatures*, Series 2, Vol. 19, No. 4 (Winter 2007), pp.143-170.

Native Origin

The old women are gathered in the Longhouse. First, the ritual kissing on the cheeks, the eyes, the lips, the top of the head; that spot where the hair parts in the middle like a wild river through a canyon.

A Grandmother sets the pot over the fire that has never gone out. To let the flames die is a taboo, a break of trust. The acorn shells have been roasted the night before. Grandmother pours the boiling water over the shells. An aroma rises and combines with the smell of wood smoke, sweat, and the sharp-sweet odor of blood.

The acorn coffee steeps and grows strong and dark. The old women sit patiently in a circle, not speaking. Each set of eyes stares sharply into the air or the fire. Occasionally, a sigh is let loose from an open mouth. A Grandmother has a twitch in the corner of her eye. She rubs her nose, then smooths her hair.

The coffee is ready. Cups are brought from a wooden cupboard. Each woman is given the steaming brew. They blow on the swirling liquid, then slurp the drink into hungry mouths. It tastes good. Hot, dark, strong. A little bitter, but that is all to the good.

The women begin talking among themselves. They are together to perform a ceremony. Rituals of old women take time. There is no hurry.

The magic things are brought out from pockets and pouches.

A turtle rattle made from a she-turtle who was a companion of the woman's mother. It died the night she died, both of them ancient and tough. Now, the daughter shakes the rattle, and mother and she-turtle live again.

A bundle containing a feather from a hermit thrush. This is a holy feather. Of all the birds in the sky, hermit thrush is the one who flew to the Spirit World. It was there she learned her beautiful song. She is clever and hides from sight. To have her feather is great magic. The women pass the feather. They tickle each other's chins and ears. Giggles and laughter erupt in the dwelling.

Bundles of corn, kernels of red, yellow, black. These also are passed from wrinkled hand to dry palm. Each woman holds the corn in her hand for a while before giving it to her sister.

Leaves of Witch Hazel and Jewelweed. Dandelion roots for chewing. Pearly Everlasting for smoking. These things are given careful attention. Much talk is generated over the old ways of preparing these gifts.

A woman gives a smile and brings a cradleboard from behind her back. There is nodding of heads and laughter and long drawn-out "ahhhhhs." The cradleboard has a beaded back that a mother made in her ninth month. An old woman starts a song; the others join her:

Little baby
Little baby
Ride on Mother's back
Laugh, laugh
Life is good
Mother shields you
Mother shields you.

A Grandmother wipes her eyes, another holds her hands and kisses the lifelines.

Inside the cradleboard are bunches of moss taken from a menstrual house. This moss has staunched lakes of blood that generations of women have squeezed from their wombs.

The acorn drink is reheated and passed once more. A woman adds wood to the fire. She holds her arms out to the flames. Another woman comes behind her with a warm blanket. She wraps it around her friend and hugs her shoulders. They stand before the fire.

A pelt of fur is brought forth. It once belonged to a beaver. She was found one morning, frozen in the ice, her lodge unfinished. The beaver was thawed and skinned. The women worked the hide until it was soft and pliant. It was the right size to wrap a newborn in, or to comfort old women on cold nights.

A piece of flint. An eagle bone whistle. A hank of black hair, cut in mourning. These are examined with reverence. The oldest Grandmother removes a pouch from around her neck. She opens it with rusty fingers. She spreads the contents in her lap. A fistful of dark earth. It smells clean, fecund. The women inhale the odor. The metallic taste of iron is on their tongues, like a sting. The oldest Grandmother scoops the earth back into her pouch. She tugs at the string. It closes. The pouch lies between her breasts, warming her skin. Her breasts are supple and soft for one so old. Not long ago, she nursed a sister back to health. A child drank from her and was healed of evil spirits that entered her as she lay innocent and dreaming.

The ceremony is over. The magic things are put in their places. The women kiss and touch each other's faces. They go out into the night. The moon and stars are parts of Sky Woman. She glows—never dimming, never retreating.

The Grandmothers gather inside the Longhouse. They tend to the fire.

Mohawk Trail

There is a small body of water in Canada called the Bay of Quinte. Look for three pine trees gnarled and entwined together. Woodland Indians, they call the people who live here. This is a reserve of Mohawks, the People of the Flint. On this reserve lived a woman of the Turtle Clan. Her name was Eliza, and she had many children. Her daughters bore flower names—Pansy, Daisy, Ivy, and Margaret Rose.

Margaret grew up, married Joseph of the Wolf Clan. They had a son. He was Joseph, too. Eight children later, they moved to Detroit, America. More opportunities for Margaret's children. Grandpa Joseph took a mail-order course in drafting. He thought Detroit would educate his Turtle children. It did.

Joseph, the son, met a white woman. Her name is Hazel. Together, they made me. All of Margaret's children married white. So, the children of Margaret's children are different. Half-blood. "Half-breed," Uncle Doug used to tease. But he smiled as he said it. Uncle was a musician and played jazz. They called him Red. Every Christmas Eve, Uncle phoned us kids and pretended he was Santa. He asked, "Were you good little Indians or bad little Indians?" We, of course, would tell tales of our goodness to our mothers and grandmother. Uncle signed off with a "ho ho ho" and a shake of his turtle rattle. Uncle died from alcohol. He was buried in a shiny black suit, his rattle in his hands, and a beaded turtle around his neck.

Some of my aunts went to college. Grandma baked pies and bread for Grandpa to sell in the neighborhood. It helped to pay for precious education. All of my aunts had skills, had jobs. Shirley became a dietician and cooked meals for kids in school. She was the first Indian in the state of Michigan to get that degree. She was very proud of what she had done for The People. Laura was a secretary. She received a plaque one year from her boss, proclaiming her speed at typing. Someone had painted a picture of an Indian in headdress typing furiously. Laura was supposed to laugh but she didn't. She quit instead. Hazel could do anything. She worked as a cook, as a clerk in a five and ten-cent store. She made jewelry out of shells and stones and sold them door to door. Hazel was the first divorcee in our family. It was thrilling to be the niece of a woman so bold. Elsie was a sickly girl. She didn't go to school and worked in a grocery store, minded women's children for extra money. She caught the streetcar in winter, bundled in Grandma's coat and wearing bits of warmth from her sisters' wardrobes. When she died, it wasn't from consumption or influenza. She died from eight children and cancer of the womb and breast. Colleen became a civil servant, serving the public, selling stamps over the counter.

After marrying white men, my aunts retired their jobs. They became secret artists, putting up huge amounts of quilts, needle work, and beadwork in the fruit cellars. Sometimes, when husbands and children slept, the aunts slipped into the cellars and gazed at their work. Smoothing an imaginary wrinkle from a quilt, running the embroidery silks through their roughened fingers, threading the beads on a small loom, working the red, blue, and yellow stones. By day, the dutiful wife. By night, sewing and beading their souls into beauty that will be left behind after death, telling the stories of who these women were.

My dad worked in a factory, making cars he never drove. Mama encouraged dad to go to school. Grandma prayed he would go to school. Between the two forces, Daddy decided to make cars in the morning and go to college at night. Mama took care of children for money. Daddy went to school for years. He eventually became a quiet teacher. He loved his work. His ambition, his dream, was to teach on a reservation. There were so many debts from school. We wore hand-me-downs most of our young lives. Daddy had one suit to teach in. When he wore his beaded necklace, some of the students laughed. His retirement came earlier than expected. The white boys in his Indian History class beat him up as they chanted, "Injun Joe, Injun Joe." My mama stopped taking care of children. Now she takes care of Daddy and passes on the family lore to me.

When I was a little girl, Grandpa taught me Mohawk. He thought I was smart. I thought he was magic. He had a special room that was filled with blueprints. When and if he had a job, he'd get out the exotic paper, and I sat very still, watching him work. As he worked, he told me stories. His room smelled of ink, tobacco, and sometimes, forbidden whiskey. Those times were good when I was a little girl. When Grandpa died, I forgot the language. But in my dreams I remember—*raksotha raoka: ra'*.[1]

Margaret had braids that wrapped around her head. It was my delight to unbraid them every night. I would move the brush from the top of her head down through the abundance of silver that was her hair. Once, I brought her hair up to my face. She smelled like smoke and woods. Her eyes were smoke also. Secret fires, banked down. I asked her to tell me about the reserve, She told me her baby had died there, my father's twin. She told me about Eliza. Eliza had dreams of her family flying in the air, becoming seeds that sprouted on new ground. The earth is a turtle where new roots bear new fruit. "Eliza gave me life," Grandma said. Grandmother, you have given me my life.

Late at night, pulling the quilt up to cover me, she whispered, "Don't forget who you are. Don't ever leave your family. They are what matters."

---

1 my grandfather's story

For All My Grandmothers

A hairnet covered her head
a net
encasing the silver
a cage
confining the wildness.
No thread escaped.

Once, hair spilling,
you ran through the woods
hair catching on branches
filaments gathered leaves
burrs attached to you.
You sang.
Your bare feet skimmed the earth.

Prematurely taken from the land
giving birth to children
who grew in a world that is white.
Prematurely
you put your hair up
covered it with a net.

Prematurely grey
they called it.

Hairbinding.

Damming the flow.

With no words, quietly
the hair fell out
formed webs on the dresser
on the pillow
in your brush.
These tangled strands pushed to the back of a drawer

wait for me to untangle
to comb through
to weave the split fibers
and make a material
strong enough
to encompass our lives.

Coyote Learns a New Trick

Coyote thought of a good joke.

She laughed so hard, she almost wanted to keep it to herself. But what good is a joke if you can't trick creatures into believing one thing is true when Coyote knows truth is only what she makes it.

She laughed and snorted and got out her sewing machine and made herself a wonderful outfit. Brown tweed pants with a zipper in the front and very pegged bottoms. A white shirt with pointed collar and french cuffs. A tie from a scrap of brown and black striped silk she had found in her night rummagings. She had some brown cowboy boots in her closet and spit on them, polishing them with her tail. She found some pretty stones that she fashioned into cufflinks for her dress shirt.

She bound her breasts with an old diaper left over from her last litter, and placed over this a sleeveless undershirt that someone had thrown in the garbage dump. It had a few holes and smelled strong, but that went with the trick. She buttoned the white shirt over the holes and smell, and wound the tie around her neck where she knotted it with flair.

She stuffed more diapers into her underpants so it looked like she had a swell inside. A big swell.

She was almost ready, but needed something to hide her brown hair. Then she remembered a fedora that had been abandoned by an old friend, and set it at an angle over one brown eye.

She looked in the mirror and almost died laughing. She looked like a very dapper male of style.

Out of her bag of tricks, she pulled a long silver chain and looped it from her belt to her pocket, where it swayed so fine.

Stepping outside her lair, she told her pups she'd be back after she had performed this latest bit of magic. They waved her away with, "Oh Mom, what is it this time?"

Subduing her laughter, she walked slowly, wanting each creature to see her movements and behold the wondrous Coyote strutting along.

A hawk spied her, stopped in mid-circle, then flew down to get a good look. "My god, I've never seen anything like it!" And Hawk screamed and carried on, her wing beating her leg as she slapped it with each whoop of laughter. Then she flew back into the sky in hot pursuit of a juicy rat she had seen earlier.

Coyote was undaunted. She knew she looked good, and besides, hawks have been known to have no sense of humor.

Dancing along, Coyote saw Turtle, as usual, caught between the road and the marsh. Stepping more quickly, Coyote approached Turtle and asked, in a sarcastic manner, if Turtle needed directions. Turtle fixed her with an astonished eye and hurriedly moved towards the weeds, grumbling about creatures who were too weird to *even* bother with.

Coyote's plan was not going so well.

Then she thought of Fox. That la-di-da female who was forever grooming her pelt and telling stories about how clever and sly she was. "She's the one!" said Coyote.

So she sauntered up to Fox's place, whistling and perfecting her new deep voice and showful walk. Knocking on Fox's door, she brushed lint and hairs from her shirt, and crushed the hat more securely on her head. Fox opened the door, and her eyes got very large with surprise and admiration.

"Can I help you?" she said with a brush of her eyelashes.

Coyote said, "I seem to be lost. Can you tell a man like me where to find a dinner to refresh myself after my long walk?"

Fox said, "Come on in. I was just this minute fixing a little supper and getting ready to have something cool to drink. Won't you join me? It wouldn't do for a stranger to pass through my place and not feel welcomed."

Coyote was impressed. This was going better than she had planned. She stifled a laugh.

"Did you say something?" Fox seemed eager to know.

"I was just admiring your red fur. Mighty pretty."

"Oh, it's nothing. Inherited you know. But I really stand in admiration of your hat and silver chain. Where did you ever find such things?"

"Well, I'm a traveling man myself. Pick up things here and there. Travel mostly at night. You can find a lot of things at night. It sure smells good in here. You must be a fine cook."

Fox laughed, "I've been known to cook up a few things. Food is one of the more sensual pleasures in life, don't you think?" she said, pouring Coyote a glass of red wine. "But I can think of several things that are equally as pleasurable, can't you?" And she winked her red eye. Coyote almost choked on her wine. She realized that she had to get this joke back into her own paws.

"Say, you're a pretty female. Got a man around the house?" Fox laughed and laughed and laughed, her red fur shaking.

"No, there are no men around her. Just me and sometimes a few girlfriends that stay over." And Fox laughed and laughed and laughed, her long nose sniffing and snorting.

Coyote couldn't figure out why Fox laughed so much. Maybe she was nervous with such a fine-looking Coyote in her house. Why, I bet she's never seen the likes of me! But it's time to get on with the trick.

Now, Coyote's trick was to make a fool out of Fox. To get her all worked up, thinking Coyote was a male, then reveal her true female Coyote self. It would make a good story. How Fox thought she was so sly and smart, but a Coyote got the best of her. Why, Coyote could tell this story for years to come!

One thing led to another, as they often do. They ate dinner, drank a little more red wine. Fox batted her eyelashes so much, Coyote thought they'd fall off! But Coyote was having a good time too. Now was the time.

"Hey Fox, you seem like a friendly type. How about a roll in the hay?"

"I thought you'd never ask," said Fox, laughing and laughing.

Lying on Fox's pallet, having her body next to hers, Coyote thought maybe she'd wait a bit before playing the trick. Besides, it was fun to be rolling around with a red-haired female. And man oh man, she really could kiss. That tongue of hers sure knows a trick or two. And boy oh boy, that sure feels good, her paw on my back, rubbing and petting. And wow, I never knew foxes could do such things, moving her legs like that, pulling me down on top of her like that. And she makes such pretty noises, moaning like that. And her paw feels real good, unzipping my pants. And oh oh, she's going to find out the trick, and then what'll I do?

"Coyote! Why don't you take that ridiculous stuffing out of your pants. And take off that undershirt, it smells to high heaven. And let me untie that binder so we can get down to *serious* business."

Coyote had not fooled Fox. But somehow, playing the trick didn't seem so important anyway.

So Coyote took off her clothes, laid on top of Fox, her leg moving between Fox's open limbs. She panted and moved and panted some more and told herself that foxes were clever after all. In fact, they were downright smart with all the stuff they knew.

Mmmmm yeah, this Fox is pretty clever with all the stuff she knows. This is the best trick I ever heard of. Why didn't I think of it?

Garnet Lee

"Honey, I was born in Kentucky fifty-six years ago.

Daddy worked in the coal mines. Mommy did cleanin' for the coal mine owners. You could say we was a company family. You could say that.

There was nine of us kids. It were hard on Mommy and Daddy.

When I was a kid, I didn't hold much with learnin'. Mommy was all the time preachin' on us that we needed an education. That it were a one-way ticket outta Grassman's Gulch. Grassman's Gulch, that's where I'm from. The best thing about school was the readin'. We didn't have no libraries, but this lady that were my teacher, well she had millions a books up to her place. She invited some of us up and said we could borrow them. Honey, the books I borrowed woulda filled a house! I was all the time readin'.

I remember this here one about a English lady, name of Jane Eyre. I can remember thinkin', why Garnet Lee, you ain't got it so bad. Leastwise, you got you a mommy and a daddy, and this here little English lady was a orphan. And that were a hundred years ago and things not as easy as they is now. That book stuck in me. Musta read it one hundred times!

In school, like I say, I liked the readin' part. But that other stuff. Lordy, I was thinkin' I must be some kind a dummy!

But I finished my education. On Graduation Day I says to Mommy, 'Well Mommy, where's my one-way ticket outta here?' She and Daddy laughed, fit to kill!

Later on, I was sorry I said what I said after what happened to my daddy. See, Daddy had the black lung. He knew it. Most everybody what worked in the mines had it. But it weren't the black lung got him. It were the explosion.

It seemed like we was always waitin' on that siren to go off. And when it did, you could see the same look passin' over folks' faces—scared to death it were gonna be our daddies or husbands killed.

That's how my daddy died.

When they brought him up from the mine, I thought Mommy was goin' to lose her mind! He were covered in coal dust, and Mommy was a screamin' and a cursin'. 'Wipe that dust offen my man's face, cain't you see he cain't breathe! He gonna die iffen he cain't breathe!'

And she kept on screamin' his name, 'Lewis Joe! Lewis Joe!' And me bein' the oldest, I couldn't bring my daddy back, and I stood with my arms around my mommy thinkin', Sweet Jesus, how'm I gonna take care of us all? I knowed that were what Mommy was thinkin'. If she could even think beyond that tore-up feeling she had inside.

The women folk, they took the kids for the night. Me and Mommy went back to our place, and some of the ladies stayed with us.

Mommy keened most a the night. In my wildest nightmares I hear that cry that don't sound like nothin' human.

We didn't have no insurance. And the company tried to buy off the relations of the dead men with a compensation. One hundred dollars.

They brought that old envelope up to the house and Mommy opened it and said, 'You mean my man was only worth a hundred dollars? Look again, you thievin' murderers!' And she tore that hundred dollar bill right in little pieces and threw it in Mr. Harry Bridgewater's face. I was right proud of Mommy. She looked a fright. Like some haint from down the gulch, her skinny little body just a shakin', and her fists right up to Mr. Bridgewater's nose. That black hair of hers, just a standin' out like a wild woman.

She slammed the door on the company, then says to us kids, 'Listen kids, we goin' to Detroit, Michigan where Aunt May lives. She got her a big heart, and I hope she got even a bigger house, cause we a movin' in!'

Now I was seventeen at the time. With a high school education. Most girls I knew were already married and havin' kids. I was right glad that hadn't happened to me. So I thought, Detroit, here I come, and you better be ready for Garnet Lee Taylor!

I'd been workin' since I was twelve, washin' laundry, cleanin' houses. Even had a little savin's account. Mommy always said I should put some money aside for myself. Said it made a girl proud to have a few dollars to her name. And I was a proud one, sure enough.

We used that money to take the train to Detroit. Lord, that was a trip! Mommy looked real old and tired. She were only thirty-three years old and a old woman afore her time. I swore I was gonna get me a job in one a them factories I heard about and make me some good money. For Mommy and the kids.

We moved to Aunt May's. You know they just welcomed us and made it feel like it were our home too. Mommy looked for work every day. But who was goin' to hire a woman that looked a hundred years old? I only saw Mommy laugh onct or twict while we was livin' at Aunt May's.

But I got a job! Workin' for Chrysler's. I couldn't believe my luck. Them days, they had so many women workin' the factories, because of the way, they didn't want no more. But my cousin Bobby, he was in the union and talked to them high-up people, and they hired me on. It like to kill me! Girl, if there ever was a tired woman, it was me. I'd always worked hard, but this was different. The noise was so bad. I thought my eardrums would bust. And everything just moved by so fast. I was scared silly. Thought I'd lose my hearin', then my arm.

Them days, there were a big war effort goin' on. I had to learn all kinda things havin' to do with machines. Lordy, I cut myself up some, and not a soul would help me. But I said, 'Garnet Lee Taylor, if you can't do what a bunch a men can do, then you ain't worth your salit.' I was young and healthy. Even had all my teeth then! I made it through, like I knew I would. The men, they called me 'hillbilly,' then wanted to come callin' on me! I said, 'Listen boys, you make a insult with one hand, then hold sugar in the other. Which one *am* I supposed to take?!'

After the war, they wanted to get rid of the ladies right quick. But I stuck to my rights. I belonged to the union by then. My proudest day was when I got my union card. Girl, the U.A.W.!! My daddy died for lack of a union. Garnet Lee Taylor was not goin' to die or be put outta a job. I had a family to raise, just like any man, and they was dependent on me and my job.

I moved Mommy and the kids into a apartment in Hamtramck, not far from the plant. I could walk to work, and we'd save that little extra for the kids' education. Some a the older ones was gettin' restless. You know boys, they wanted to be on their own. But I told them, 'You get you a job and finish that education or you don't come runnin' to me and Mommy for to get you back on your feet!' They was all good kids. Daddy and Mommy did a decent upbringin' on us. The boys got steady jobs. So did the girls. And they weren't no tramps neither! It's funny how when people hear your accent, they think you're trash and treat you like their garbage don't stink same as yours. Some a them northerners was a funny bunch!

I worked side by side a colored man for fifteen years. I learned some by doin' that. Yes, Samuel was a learner to me. Now, work is work, and if you're workin' and doin' what you're supposed to, you ain't got time for that name calling and prejudice stuff. But there were always some didn't like Samuel nor the other colored folk. Just cause their skin was black. Actually, Samuel was a brown man. Brown like the garden dirt, right before spring. Dark and true. I miss that man. He died some years back. Some a his kids workin' at the plant now. I say, if you work with a person long enough, you're just a plain fool if you can't see you're in it together. Workin' people's lives is hard times. You got to stick to each other. It's like bein' in a family. Lord knows, families can be a pain in the you-know-what, but nothin' ain't easy. Yes, workin' people got to stick to each other. Lord knows, the company ain't goin' to!

It seemed like the years just flew away. Pretty soon, there were just Mommy and me. Why, Betty Opal and Louise even went to college. Lewis, Ruth, and Chrystal moved back home. Lew's workin' in the same mine our daddy died in. But Lew's got hisself a union. Ain't nobody goin' to mess with him! I hear they even got women a workin' them mines. Lordy be, my heart goes out to them ladies. I know it must be hard. Wasn't it hard on all us ladies? But you know girl, I always did have a big mouth and a don't-you-mess-in-my-business attitude.

Men. I've had plenty in my life and plenty is more than I needed! But my women friends, now that's another story. I don't have to tell you that when it come to bein' friends, real buddies, ain't nothin' like a woman to help you get over the sorrows of livin'. We have some good times, let me tell you. I'd say that women folk got somethin' special. Tenderness. We can be mean as snakes and then some, but the women, well we got a tender quality too. A right sweetness.

When the plant closed in Hamtramck, I was transferred over here. So me and Mommy bought this here little house in Melvindale. We even got us a back yard so's we can grow our flowers and vegetables.

Me, I'm still readin'. Even got me my own copy of Jane Eyre! Mommy says, 'Garnet Lee, we gonna have to move again, to accommodate all these books of yourn.' I just laugh and say, 'Now listen here Mommy, they be wantin' me to retire soon, and we goin' to be two old ladies gettin' in each other's hair. If I don't have my books, I'd just be worryin' you to death. So you go dig in the dirt or watch that twenty-four inch color TV you got. Don't you be teasin' me none about my recreation.'

Mommy come over and kiss me on the cheek and say, 'Honey, you are a right good girl. I be ever so proud a you and your book readin'.'

Tenderness. That's what I'm a talkin' about. You can't say the women ain't got it. You can't never say that."

Danny

"My dad worked for Ford's. What else do people do around here? Ma worked as a waitress. Man, she'd come home so fucked over and tired, I used to want to jill! Guys all the time putting the make on her. Ma was real pretty, and Dad was jealous. I could hear them fight when I was a kid. Me and Sean and Joey would hear him yelling at her, saying she was coming on to the men in the diner. But she wasn't. She was just real pretty. It seems like when you're a kid, you gotta take sides sometimes. I always took Ma's side.

I was a pretty kid. Wanted to be like my ma. Wanted to be a girl. Sean teased me a lot, called me 'sissy.' But Joey stood up for me. Man, I loved Joey so much. He was everything a kid should be. He was strong and good in sports. But he had this sweet side to him. He used to cry when Dad got on my case about something. And that was a lot.

In a way, I couldn't blame Dad. Christ, he worked like a dog for Mr. Henry Ford so Mr. Henry Ford could live in Grosse Pointe, and have fancy houses all over the world, and be a big man. Dad thought he wasn't a man. That's why he pushed us around. Made him feel like somebody. Shit man, here we were, living in a crummy house in Lincoln Park, trying to take care of our lives. And some people on the street still talking like it was a century ago–calling us 'dirty Irish,' 'shanty pigs.' Man, I just couldn't relate to any of it. There was always so much ugliness, you know?

Early on, I liked to dress in Ma's clothes. I guess I knew it was something I shouldn't be doing, but I wanted to be pretty and dressing up made me feel pretty. I got caught once. Dad gave me a big talk about being a man. Then he beat the shit outta me to prove his point. Ma, well she asked me why I was doing it. I couldn't answer her because I didn't know.

By the time I got to high school, I was a real hippie. Wore my hair long and in a braid. God, the shit really flew! Dad threatening to throw me out of the house, calling me a 'bum,' Joey trying to make peace all the time. Ma asking me if I wanted to see a psychiatrist.

Man, she could hardly spell it, let alone know what they were for! Ma, she tried so hard with me.

Me, I talked trash to my folks and told them all to fuck off.

I took a lot of drugs. Man, there wasn't anything I wouldn't try. Christ, I couldn't make it in school if I wasn't stoned all the time.

I liked guys. Used to dream about them. It never failed, I always went for the butch types. You know, football players, jock types. But they were too busy proving what men they were—fucking girls, then bragging about it.

I moved out when I was sixteen. Moved in with Joey, who was nineteen and working in a garage. I had a job after school cutting up vegetables for this Italian restaurant. I got to eat whatever I wanted, and the old lady who owned the place really liked me. She used to tell me I was a good boy. Jesus, if only she knew what a pervert I was.

Somehow, I kept in school till I graduated. Then I thought that what I really wanted to do was to be a nurse. Working-class dreams!

I enrolled in this program. Got some loans. Joey and Ma gave me some money. The old man thought I had really gone off the deep end with this one. But hell, it was a job and a job that paid off in some ways. Or at least that's what I thought.

I was the only man in the program. But it was okay. I always liked being with women, but I knew they'd think I was a freak if they ever saw me in the dress I used to wear at night.

Finally, I became a nurse. Got my job at Children's Hospital working in the Emergency Room. Nothing prepared me for what I saw in the E.R. Little kids all beat up from their fucker fathers. Little girls bleeding and dying from some bastard's prick.

God, I hated being a man, if that's what men were!

I met my first boyfriend at the hospital. He worked in x-ray. A real sweet guy. Reminded me of Joey. We wanted to live together, but it didn't work out. He didn't like that I wanted to dress like a woman sometimes. Said it made him feel funny. I could dig it, but it's like I *had* to do it, you know?

I sort of decided that I'd just do my thing and do my work, and life would just go along. So that's what I did.

On my nights off, I'd dress up and go down to the Corridor and parade myself. And it really was a parade. Freaks on display. Danny, the biggest freak of all. You know, there were some real sickos down there. Straight-looking guys in business suits picking up queers like me. They weren't honest, you know?

I could see myself as an old man doing this, and it scared the shit out of me. That's when I started thinking I wouldn't live to be thirty. I couldn't see any other kind of life for me.

I worked hard at the hospital. See, I liked the kids. Wanted to take the hurt away. Sometimes, I'd see the same kids over and over. We'd patch them up and the hospital would let them go back to their fucked-up lives.

Man, I wanted to blow up the world! And all the goddamn fucking bastards with it!

I used to take Valium after work to calm myself down. I stole an IV and gave it to myself that way. I'd watch it drip into my veins and think each drop was some kid's life. Crazy, huh?

The last night of my life, I got this idea to dress up in my red dress and go to the Interchange. What the fuck! It was my life, right?

At the funeral parlor, they cut my hair off, but that night it was still long. I didn't need to wear wigs like some of the boys. I was wearing those turquoise earrings you gave me. I hope you got them back. One crazy night I wrote down everything I wanted my friends to have. Joey got my guitar.

Maybe I did know something would happen to me. Man, I was so full of junk and shit, I couldn't tell whether or not I was dead or alive anyway.

I went to the Interchange. Picked up a queer. We were leaving the bar when these two dudes stopped us. The one says, 'Hey, we're the vice squad, let me see your wallet.' Shit, now I knew these dudes weren't the cops, just some kids hassling queers.

So I says, like the asshole I am, 'Get lost fucker. If you want my money, you'll have to kill me.'

The last thing I remember was him pulling out a gun and aiming it at my crotch. Then he shot me. Blew me away. For good measure, he put a bullet in my head. Wanted to make sure the freak was put away.

So, there's one less queer on the streets, and I guess that means that respectable people are resting easier in their lives. Or, most likely, they don't even know I'm gone."

Her Name is Helen

Her name is Helen.
She came from Washington State twenty years ago through
                                        broken routes
of Hollywood, California,
Gallup, New Mexico,
Las Vegas, Nevada,
ended up in Detroit, Michigan where she lives in #413
in the gut of the city.
She worked in a factory for ten years, six months, making
                                        carburetors for Cadillacs.
She loved factory work.
She made good money, took vacations to New Orleans,
"A real party town."

She wears a cowboy hat with pretty feathers.
Can't wear cowboy boots because of the arthritis that twists
                                        her feet.
She wears beige vinyl wedgies. In the winter she pulls on heavy
socks to protect her bent toes from the slush and rain.

Helen takes pictures of herself.

Everytime she passes those Polaroid booths,
one picture for a dollar,
she closes the curtain and the camera flashes.

When she was laid off from the factory
she got a job in a bar, serving up shots and beer.
Instead of tips, she gets presents from her customers.
Little wooden statues of Indians in headdress.
Naked pictures of squaws with braided hair.
Feather roach clips in fuschia and chartreuse.
Everybody loves Helen.
She's such a good guy. An honest-to-god Indian.

Helen doesn't kiss.
She allows her body to be held when she's had enough vodkas
                                            and Lite beer.
She's had lots of girlfriends.
White women who wanted to take care of her,
who liked Indians,
who think she's a tragedy.

Helen takes pictures of herself.

She has a picture on a keychain, along with a baby's shoe and a
                                            feathered roach clip.
She wears her keys on a leather belt.
Helen sounds like a chime, moving behind the bar.

Her girlfriends took care of her.
Told her what to wear
what to say
how to act more like an Indian.
"You should be proud of your Indian heritage.
Wear more jewelry.
Go to the Indian Center."

Helen doesn't talk much.
Except when she's had enough
vodkas and Lite beer.
Then she talks about home,
about her mom,
about the boarding schools,
the foster homes,
about wanting to go back to see her people
before she dies.
Helen says she's going to die when she's fifty.

She's forty-two now.
Eight years to go.

Helen doesn't kiss.
Doesn't talk much.
Takes pictures of herself.

She touches women who are white.
She is touched by their hands.

Helen can't imagine that she is beautiful.
That her skin is warm
like redwood and fire.
That her thick black hair moves like a current.
That her large body speaks in languages stolen from her.
That her mouth is wide and full and when she smiles
people catch their breath.

"I'm a gay Indian girl.
A dumb Indian.
A fat, ugly squaw."
This is what Helen says.

She wears a t-shirt with the legend
Detroit
splashed in glitter across her large breasts.
Her breasts that white women have sucked and molded to fit
their mouths.

Helen can't imagine that there are women
who see her.
That there are women
who want to taste her breath and salt.
Who want a speech to be created between their tongues.
Who want to go deep inside her
touch places that are dark, wet,
muscle and spirit.
Who want to swell, expand two bodies into a word of our own
making.

Helen can't imagine that she is beautiful.

She doesn't kiss.
Doesn't talk much.
Takes pictures of herself so she will know she is there.

Takes pictures of herself to prove she is alive.

Helen takes pictures of herself.

A Long Story

Dedicated to my Great-Grandmothers
Eliza Powless and Catherine Brant

"About 40 Indian children took the train at this depot for the Philadelphia Indian School last Friday. They were accompanied by the government agent, and seemed a bright looking lot."

The Northern Observer
(Massena, New York, July 20, 1892)

"I am only beginning to understand what it means for a mother to lose a child."

Anna Demeter, *Legal Kidnapping*
(Beacon Press, Boston, 1977)

1890

It has been two days since they came and took the children away. My body is greatly chilled. All our blankets have been used to bring me warmth. The women keep the fire blazing. The men sit. They talk among themselves. We are frightened by this sudden child-stealing. We signed papers, the agent said. This gave them rights to take our babies. It is good for them, the agent said. It will make them civilized, the agent said. I do not know *civilized*.

I hold myself tight in fear of flying apart in the air. The others try to feed me. Can they feed a dead woman? I have stopped talking. When my mouth opens, only air escapes. I have used up my sound screaming their names—She Sees Deer! He Catches The Leaves! My eyes stare at the room, the walls of scrubbed wood, the floor of dirt. I know there are people here, but I cannot see them. I see a darkness, like the lake at New Moon. Black, unmoving in the center, a picture of my son and daughter being lifted onto the train. My daughter wearing the dark blue, heavy dress. All of the girls dressed alike. Never have I seen such eyes! They burn into my head even now. My son. His hair cut. Dressed as the white men, his arms and legs covered by cloth that made him sweat. His face, streaked with tears. So many children crying, screaming. The sun on our bodies, our heads. The train screeching like a crow, sounding like laughter. Smoke and dirt pumping out of the insides of the train. So many people. So many children. The women, standing as if in prayer, our hands lifted, reaching. The dust sifting down on our palms. Our palms making motions at the sky. Our fingers closing like the claws of the bear.

I see this now. The hair of my son held in my hands. I rub the strands, the heavy braids coming alive as the fire flares and casts a bright light on the black hair. They slip from my fingers and lie coiled on the ground. I see this. My husband picks up the braids, wraps them in cloth; he takes the pieces of our son away. He walks outside, the eyes of the people on him. I see this. He will find a bottle and drink with the men. Some of the women will join him. They will end the night by singing or crying. It is all the same. I see this. No sounds of children playing games and laughing. Even the dogs have ceased their noise. They lay outside each doorway, waiting. I hear this. The voices of children. They cry. They pray. They call me. *Nisten ha.* I hear this. *Nisten ha.*[1]

1978

I am wakened by the dream. In the dream my daughter is dead. Her father is returning her body to me in pieces. He keeps her heart. I thought I screamed . . . *Patricia!* I sit up in bed, swallowing air as if for nourishment. The dream remains in the air. I rise to go to her room. Ellen tries to lead me back to bed, but I have to see once again. I open her door. She is gone. The room empty, lonely. They said it was in her best interests, How can that be? She is only six, a baby who needs her mothers. She loves us. This has not happened. I will not believe this. Oh god, I think I have died.

---

1 mother

Night after night, Ellen holds me as I shake. Our sobs stifling the air in our room. We lie in our bed and try to give comfort. My mind can't think beyond last week when she left. I would have killed him if I'd had the chance! He took her hand and pulled her to the car. The look in his eyes of triumph. It was a contest to him, Patricia the prize. He will teach her to hate us. He will! I see her dear face. That face looking out the back window of his car. Her mouth forming the words *Mommy, Mama.* Her dark braids tied with red yarn. Her front teeth missing. Her overalls with the yellow flower on the pocket, embroidered by Ellen's hands. So lovingly she sewed the yellow wool. Patricia waiting quietly until she was finished. Ellen promising to teach her designs—chain stitch, french knot, split stitch. How Patricia told everyone that Ellen made the flower just for her. So proud of her overalls.

I open the closet door. Almost everything is gone. A few things hang there limp, abandoned. I pull a blue dress from the hanger and take it back to my room. Ellen tries to take it from me, but I hold on, the soft blue cotton smelling of my daughter. How is it possible to feel such pain and live? "Ellen?!" She croons my name. "Mary, Mary, I love you." She sings me to sleep.

1890

The agent was here to deliver a letter. I screamed at him and sent curses his way. I threw dirt in his face as he mounted his horse. He thinks I'm a crazy woman and warns me, "You better settle down Annie." What can they do to me? I am a crazy woman. This letter hurts my hand. It is written in their hateful language. It is evil, but there is a message for me.

I start the walk up the road to my brother. He works for the whites and understands their meanings. I think about my brother as I pull the shawl closer to my body. It is cold now. Soon there will be snow. The corn has been dried and hangs from our cabin, waiting to be used. The corn never changes. My brother is changed. He says that *I* have changed and bring shame to our clan. He says I should accept the fate. But I do not believe in the fate of child-stealing. There is evil here. There is much wrong in our village. My brother says I am a crazy woman because I howl at the sky every evening. He is a fool. I am calling the children. He says the people are becoming afraid of me because I talk to the air and laugh like the raven overhead. But I am talking to the children. They need to hear the sound of me. I laugh to cheer them. They cry for us.

This letter burns my hands. I hurry to my brother. He has taken the sign of the wolf from over the doorway. He pretends to be like those who hate us. He gets more and more like the child-stealers. His eyes move away from mine. He takes the letter from me and begins the reading of it. I am confused. This letter is from two strangers with the names Martha and Daniel. They say they are learning civilized ways. Daniel works in the fields, growing food for the school. Martha cooks and is being taught to sew aprons. She will be going to live with the schoolmaster's wife. She will be a live-in girl. What is a *live-in girl?* I shake my head. The words sound the same to me. I am afraid of Martha and Daniel, these strangers who know my name. My hands and arms are becoming numb.

I tear the letter from my brother's fingers. He stares at me, his eyes traitors in his face. He calls after me, "Annie! Annie!" That is not my name! I run to the road. That is not my name! There is no Martha! There is no Daniel! This is witch work. The paper burns and burns. At my cabin, I quickly dig a hole in the field. The earth is hard and cold, but I dig with my nails. I dig, my hands feeling weaker. I tear the paper and bury the scraps. As the earth drifts and settles, the names Martha and Daniel are covered. I look to the sky and find nothing but endless blue. My eyes are blinded by the color. I begin the howling.

1978

When I get home from work, there is a letter from Patricia. I make coffee and wait for Ellen, pacing the rooms of our apartment. My back is sore from the line, bending over and down, screwing the handles on the doors of the flashy cars moving by. My work protects me from questions, the guys making jokes at my expense. But some of them touch my shoulder lightly and briefly as a sign of understanding. The few women, eyes averted or smiling in sympathy. No one talks. There is no time to talk. No room to talk, the noise taking up all space and breath.

I carry the letter with me as I move from room to room. Finally I sit at the kitchen table, turning the paper around in my hands. Patricia's printing is large and uneven. The stamp has been glued on halfheartedly and is coming loose. Each time a letter arrives, I dread it, even as I long to hear from my child. I hear Ellen's key in the door. She walks into the kitchen, bringing the smell of the hospital with her. She comes toward me, her face set in new lines, her uniform crumpled and stained, her brown hair pulled back in an imitation of a french twist. She knows there is a letter. I kiss her and bring mugs of coffee to the table. We look at each other. She reaches for my hand, bringing it to her lips. Her hazel eyes are steady in her round face.

I open the letter. *Dear Mommy. I am fine. Daddy got me a new bike. My big teeth are coming in. We are going to see Grandma for my birthday. Daddy got me new shoes. Love, Patricia.* She doesn't ask about Ellen. I imagine her father standing over her, coaxing her, coaching her. The letter becomes ugly. I tear it in bits and scatter them out the window. The wind scoops the pieces into a tight fist before strewing them in the street. A car drives over the paper, shredding it to garbage and mud.

Ellen makes a garbled sound. "I'll leave. If it will make it better, I'll leave." I quickly hold her as the dusk moves into the room and covers us. "Don't leave. Don't leave." I feel her sturdy back shiver against my hands. She kisses my throat, and her arms tighten as we move closer. "Ah Mary, I love you so much." As the tears threaten our eyes, the taste of salt is on our lips and tongues. We stare into ourselves, touching the place of pain, reaching past the fear, the guilt, the anger, the loneliness.

We go to our room. It is beautiful again. I am seeing it new. The sun is barely there. The colors of cream, brown, green mixing with the wood floor. The rug with its design of wild birds. The black ash basket glowing on the dresser, holding a bouquet of dried flowers bought at a vendor's stand. I remember the old woman, laughing and speaking rapidly in Polish as she wrapped the blossoms in newspaper. Ellen undresses me as I cry. My desire for her breaking through the heartbreak we share. She pulls the covers back, smoothing the white sheets, her hands repeating the gestures done at work. She guides me onto the cool material. I watch her remove the uniform of work. An aide to nurses. A healer of spirit.

She comes to me full in flesh. My hands are taken with the curves and soft roundness of her. She covers me with the beating of her heart. The rhythm steadies me. Heat is centering me. I am grounded by the peace between us. I smile at her face above me, round like a moon, her long hair loose and touching my breasts. I take her breast in my hand, bring it to my mouth, suck her as a woman—in desire, in faith. Our bodies join. Our hair braids together on the pillow. Brown, black, silver, catching the last light of the sun. We kiss, touch, move to our place of power. Her mouth, moving over my body, stopping at curves and swells of skin, kissing, removing pain. Closer, close, together, woven, my legs are heat, the center of my soul is speaking to her, I am sliding into her, her mouth is medicine, her heart is the earth, we are dancing with flying arms, I shout, I sing, I weep salty liquid, sweet and warm it coats her throat. This is my life. I love you Ellen, I love you Mary, I love, we love.

1891

The moon is full. The air is cold. This cold strikes at my flesh as I remove my clothes and set them on fire in the withered corn field. I cut my hair, the knife sawing through the heavy mass. I bring the sharp blade to my arms, legs, and breasts. The blood trickles like small red rivers down my body. I feel nothing. I throw the tangled webs of my hair into the flames. The smell, like a burning animal, fills my nostrils. As the fire stretches to touch the stars, the people come out to watch me—the crazy woman. The ice in the air touches me.

They caught me as I tried to board the train and search for my babies. The white men tell my husband to watch me. I am dangerous. I laugh and laugh. My husband is good only for tipping bottles and swallowing anger. He looks at me, opening his mouth and making no sound. His eyes are dead. He wanders from the cabin and looks out on the corn. He whispers our names. He calls after the children. He is a dead man.

Where have they taken the children? I ask the question of each one who travels the road past our door. The women come and we talk. We ask and ask. They say there is nothing we can do. The white man is like a ghost. He slips in and out where we cannot see. Even in our dreams he comes to take away our questions. He works magic that resists our medicine. This magic has made us weak. What is the secret about them? Why do they want our children? They sent the Blackrobes many years ago to teach us new magic. It was evil! They lied and tricked us. They spoke of gods who would forgive us if we believed as they do. They brought the rum with the cross. This god is ugly! He killed our masks. He killed our men. He sends the women screaming at the moon in terror. They want our power. They take our children to remove the inside of them. Our power. They steal our food, our sacred rattle, the stories, our names. What is left?

I am a crazy woman. I look to the fire that consumes my hair and see their faces. My daughter. My son. They still cry for me, though the sound grows fainter. The wind picks up their keening and brings it to me. The sound has bored into my brain. I begin howling. At night I dare not sleep. I fear the dreams. It is too terrible, the things that happen there. Red, dark blood in my dream. Rushing for our village. The blood moves faster. There are screams of wounded people. Animals are dead, thrown in the blood stream. There is nothing left. Only the air echoing nothing. Only the earth soaking up blood, spreading it in the four directions, becoming a thing there is no name for. I stand in the field watching the fire, The People watching me. We are waiting, but the answer is not clear yet. A crazy woman. That is what they call me.

1979

After taking a morning off work to see my lawyer, I come home, not caring if I call in. Not caring, for once, at the loss in pay. Not caring. My lawyer says there is nothing more we can do. I must wait. As if there has been something other than waiting. He has custody and calls the shots. We must wait and see how long it takes for him to get tired of being a mommy and a daddy. So, I wait.

I open the door to Patricia's room. Ellen and I keep it dusted and cleaned in case my baby will be allowed to visit us. The yellow and blue walls feel like a mockery. I walk to the windows, begin to systematically tear down the curtains. I slowly start to rip the cloth apart. I enjoy hearing the sounds of destruction. Faster, I tear the material into strips. What won't come apart with my hands, I pull at with my teeth. Looking for more to destroy, I gather the sheets and bedspread in my arms and wildly shred them to pieces. Grunting and sweating, I am pushed by rage and the searing wound in my soul. Like a wolf, caught in a trap, gnawing at her own leg to set herself free, I begin to beat my breasts to deaden the pain inside. A noise gathers in my throat and finds the way out. I begin a scream that turns to howling, then becomes hoarse choking. I want to take my fists, my strong fists, my brown fists, and smash the world until it bleeds. Bleeds! And all the judges in their flapping robes, and the fathers who look for revenge, are ground, ground into dust and disappear with the wind.

The word *lesbian*. Lesbian. The word that makes them panic, makes them afraid, makes them destroy children. The word that dares them. Lesbian. *I am one.* Even for Patricia, even for her, *I will not cease to be!* As I kneel amidst the colorful scraps, Raggedy Anns smiling up at me, my chest gives a sigh. My heart slows to its normal speech. I feel the blood pumping outward to my veins, carrying nourishment and life. I strip the room naked. I close the door.

Thanks so much to Chrystos for the title.
Thanks to Gloria Anzaldúa
for encouraging the writing of this story.

A Simple Act

for Denise Dorsz

Gourds climbing the fence. Against the rusted crisscross wires, the leaves are fresh. The green, ruffled plants twine around the wood posts that need painting. The fruit of the vine hangs in irregular shapes. Some are smooth. Others bumpy and scarred. All are colors of the earth. Brown. Green. Gold.

A gourd is a hollowed-out shell, used as a utensil. I imagine women together, sitting outside the tipis and lodges, carving and scooping. Creating bowls for food. Spoons for drinking water. A simple act—requiring lifetimes to learn. At times the pods were dried and rattles made to amuse babies. Or noisemakers, to call the spirits in sorrow and celebration.

I am taking a break from my hot room, from the writing, where I dredge for ghosts. The writing that unearths pain, old memories.

I cover myself with paper, the ink making tracks, like animals who follow the scent of water past unfamiliar ground.

I invent new from the old.

STORY ONE

Sandra

In the third, fourth, and fifth grades, we were best friends. Spending nights at each other's houses, our girl bodies hugging tight. We had much in common. Our families were large and sloppy. We occupied places of honor due to our fair skin and hair. Assimilation separated us from our ancient and inherited places of home. Your Russian gave way to English. Your blonde hair and freckles a counterpoint to the darkness of eye and black hair massed and trembling around your mother's head. My blonde hair, fine and thin, my skin pink and flushed in contrast to the sleek, black hair of my aunts, my uncle, my father. Their eyes dark, hidden by folds of skin. We were anachronisms . . . except to each other. Our friendship fit us well.

We invented stories about ourselves. We were children from another planet. We were girls from an undiscovered country. We were alien beings in families that were "different." Different among the different.

Your big sister Olga wore falsies. We stole a pair from her and took turns tucking them inside our undershirts. We pretended to be big girls, kissing on the lips and touching our foam rubber breasts. Imagining what being grown meant. In the sixth and seventh grades our blood started to flow, our breasts turned into a reality of sweet flesh and waiting nipples. The place between our thighs filled with a wanting so tender, an intensity of heat from which our fingers emerged, shimmering with liquid energy, our bodies spent with the expression of our growing strength. When we began to know what this was—that it was called love—someone told on us. Told on us. Through my bedroom window where we lay on the bed, listening to the radio, stroking blonde hair, Roger, the boy next door, saw us and told on us. Our mothers were properly upset. We heard the words from them: "You can't play with each other anymore." "You should be ashamed." "WHAT WILL PEOPLE THINK?"

We fought in our separate ways. You screamed in Russian as your father hit you with his belt. You cursed him, vowing revenge. Your mother watched, painfully, but did not interfere, upholding the morality of the family. My mother shamed me by promising not to tell the rest of the family. I refused to speak to her for weeks, taking refuge in silence, the acceptable solution. I hated her for the complicity we shared.

Sandra, we couldn't help but see each other. You lived across the street. We'd catch glimpses of the other running to school. Our eyes averted, never focusing. The belt marks, the silences the shame, restoring us once again to our rightful places. We were good girls, nice girls, after all. So, like an old blouse that had become too thin and frayed, an embarrassment to wear, our friendship was put away, locked up inside our past. Entering the eighth grade in 1954, we were thirteen years old. Something hard, yet invisible, had formed over our memory. We went the way of boys, back seats of cars, self-destruction. I heard you were put in the hospital with sugar diabetes. I sent a card—unsigned. Your family moved away. I never saw you again.

Sandra, we are forty-one now.
I have three daughters.
A woman lover.
I am a writer.
Sandra, I am remembering our loss.
Sandra . . . I am remembering.
I loved you.

We have a basket filled with gourds. Your basket is woven from sweetgrass, and the scent stirs up the air and lights on our skin. This still life sits on a table in front of our bedroom window. In late afternoon, the sun glances around the hanging plants, printing designs on the wall and on our arms as we lay on our bed. We trust our love to each other's care. The room grows heavy with words. Our lungs expand to breathe the life gestating in the space connecting your eyes to mine. You put your hand on my face and imprint forever, in memory, this passage of love and faith. I watch you come from your bath. I pull you toward me, my hands soothed by the wetness on your back and between your thighs. You smell of cinnamon and clean water. Desire shapes us. Desire to touch with our hands, our eyes, our mouths, our minds. I bend over you, kissing the hollow of your throat, your pulse leaping under my lips.

We touch.

Dancers wearing shells of turtles, feathers of eagles, bones of our people.

We touch.

STORY TWO

My House

The house I grew up in was a small frame box. It had two stories. My sister, cousins, and I shared a room on the second floor. A chestnut tree rubbed its branches against our window. In the summer, we opened the glass panes and coaxed the arms of the tree into the room. Grandpa spoke to the tree every night. We listened to the words, holding our breath and our questions in fear of breaking a magic we knew was happening, but couldn't name.

In our house, we spoke the language of censure. Sentences stopped in the middle. The joke without a punch line. The mixture of a supposed-to-be-forgotten Mohawk, strangled with uneasy English.

I was a dreamer. I created places of freedom in my mind. Words that my family whispered in their sleep could be shouted. Words that we were not supposed to say could be sung, like the hymns Grandma sang on Sundays.

The secrets we held to ourselves. We swallowed them. They lay at the bottoms of our stomachs, making us fat with nerves and itching from inside.

The secrets we held to ourselves.

The secret that my mom's father refused to see her after she married a dark man, an Indian man.

The secret that my uncle drank himself to oblivion—then death.

The secret that Grandma didn't go out because storekeepers called her names—*dumb Indian, squaw.*

The secret that Grandpa carried heart inside him clogged with the starches, the fats, the poverty of food that as a young man, as an Indian, he had no choice about eating.

All of us, weighed down by invisible scales. Balancing always, our life among the assimilators and our life of memory.

We were shamed. We didn't fit. We didn't belong.

I had learned the lessons. I kept my mouth shut. I kept the quiet.

One night in August, 1954, a fire in the basement.
Things burned.

Secret things.
Indian things.
Things the neighbors never saw.
False Faces. Beaded necklaces. Old letters written in Mohawk. A turtle rattle. Corn husks.
Secrets brought from home.
Secrets protecting us in hostile places.

"Did you lose anything?" The neighbors stood, anxious to not know. The night air was hot. The moon hung full and white. The stars in a crazy design over us.
"Did you lose anything?" The question came again.
"Just a few old things". . . and Grandma and Grandpa stepped into the house, led by my mother's and father's hands. My grandparents tears were acid, tunneling holes in their cheeks.
"Don't forget this night, *kontirio.*[1] Don't forget this night."
Grandfather looked at me, the phrase repeated again and again.
"Don't forget this night."
Grandfather's back became a little more stooped. He lapsed into Mohawk at odd moments. His heart stopped in his sleep. Heavy. Constricted. Silenced.
Grandmother's back became a little thicker. Her shoulders were two eagles transfixed on a mountain, checked in flight. Her hands became large and knobby from arthritis. Still, she made the fry bread, the corn soup, the quilts, and changed the diapers of her great-grandchildren. She never spoke of that night. Her eyes faded, watery with age. She died. Her heart quitting in her sleep.
I closed the windows and covered my ears to the knocking of the tree.

In my room overlooking the back yard.
Through the open window, I smell the cut grass, hear
gourds rattle as a breeze moves along quickly, bringing
a promise of autumn and change.
I sit at the desk, pen in my hand, paper scattered underneath. Trying to bring forth sound and words.

---

1 wild animal

Unblocking my throat.
Untying my tongue.
Scraping sand from my eyes.
Pulling each finger out of the fist I have carried at
my side.
Unclenching my teeth.
Burning the brush ahead of me, brambles cutting across
my mind.
Each memory a pain in the heart. But *this* heart keeps
pumping blood through my body, keeping me alive.

I write because to not write is a breach of faith.

Out of a past where amnesia was the expected.
Out of a past occupied with quiet.
Out of a past, I make truth for a future.

Cultures gone up in flames.
The smell of burning leather, paper, flesh, filling the
spaces where memory fails.
The smell of a chestnut tree, its leaves making magic,
The smell of Sandra's hair, like dark coffee and incense.

I close my eyes. Pictures unreeling on my eyelids.
Portraits of beloved people flashing by quickly.
Opening my eyes, I think of the seemingly ordinary
things that women do. And how, with the brush of an
eyelash against a cheek, the movement of pen on paper,
power is born.

A gourd is a hollowed-out shell, used as a utensil.

We make our bowls from the stuff of nature. Of life.

We carve and scoop, discarding the pulp.

Ink on paper, picking up trails I left so many lives ago.

Leaving my mark, my footprints, my sign.

I write what I know.

Wild Turkeys

Violet smiled when she saw the sign: Welcome to Fairview, Wild Turkey Capital of Michigan. The sign had been there for as long as she could remember, the same tired old bird peering out from behind the letters. Over the years the vivid colors of the bird's feathers had dulled to a light brown, and the black lettering was now a washed-out grey. Violet had lived nearby before she ran away. But she remembered the sign and remembered the wild turkeys.

She was six or seven when she'd seen them. While playing in the field near her home, she came across them pecking for food and moving silently on the ground. She thought they were ugly birds until they spread their wings and skittered away from her. Then the rich reds, rusts, and browns were displayed for her to see. They flew low over the field, not reaching any great height, almost as if it were a struggle to get off the ground. She had run home to tell her mom about the birds. Her mom told Violet a story.

"In the old days, sweetie, the turkey used to fly real high. Almost as high as a hawk. There was an animal, a porcupine, who got jealous of the turkey's pretty colors and the way she could fly. See, the porcupine was kinda ugly. One night when the turkey was sleeping, the porcupine sneaked up and clipped her wings with his sharp claws. After that, the turkey couldn't fly very far or very high, but she still kept her pretty feathers. The porcupine made the Creator so mad, he gave him those long, sharp quills so nobody would go near him anymore."

"That's sad, Mom."

"Well, lots of things are sad, Violet. But the turkey kept her feathers and she's still alive. I think that's the important thing."

Slowing down the car to get a good look at the sign, she saw another across the street: Rita's Diner. She didn't remember the diner; it must be new. She was hungry and needed some coffee to fortify her for the two hours of driving she still had ahead of her. She pulled into the lot and sat for a few minutes, checking her money supply and cleaning her glasses. She had spent more than she'd planned on this trip back to see her grandmother. She had bought a birdhouse for Grandma who loved to sit and watch the birds that came to visit her yard. The birdhouse was a fancy one, handmade, with dozens of small holes for the birds to nest. Violet had set it up by the front window where Grandma spent most of her day, looking out at the trees and rose bushes.

"Can't you stay longer, Violet? It's been so long since I seen you. Talking on the phone's not the same as having my best girl here."

Violet had looked at her grandmother's old, lined face, the brown eyes full of life and curiosity. "I'm starting my new job tomorrow, but I promise I'll come back more often, Grandma. I'll be making more money so I can afford the travel as long as the car holds out. If it weren't for you and the money you've given me, I don't know what I would have done. But I'll be back. I'm not scared anymore."

"You shouldn't be. He's long gone, can't hurt you no more. And the money," Grandma waved away the hundreds of dollars she had sent to Violet, "what have I got to spend it on?"

"You don't have that much, Grandma."

"I don't need much. Now that I got this fancy birdhouse, I got everything I need," and she had pulled Violet to her and kissed her.

Violet had entered the diner, noting the smallness and cleanliness of the place. There were only a few tables, no booths, and the walls were painted a sun yellow. Red-and-white checked curtains hung at the scrubbed windows. She sat down at a table and looked around the space, grinning when she saw the stuffed turkey mounted on a wall. Turkeys were evident most everywhere. Turkey salt-and-pepper shakers were sitting on each table. Her napkin, aligned in front of her, had knife, fork, and spoon lying on top of a foolishly smiling turkey. There were photographs and paintings of wild turkeys hanging on the walls.

A waitress with improbable red-lacquered hair came over and poured coffee into the thick white mug resting beside the smiling turkey. Violet noticed the woman's hands were chapped and red. She looked up and smiled her thanks. The pin on the woman's yellow uniform said Rita. Violet looked around the room as she sipped her coffee. A group of men were sitting at a table by the window. Across from her, a woman was eating from a plate of french fries, her black hair pulled back into a ponytail, secured with two beaded barrettes. The woman smiled shyly at Violet and resumed eating her fries.

"You hear about Rosie?" the waitress inquired to no one in particular. "After all these years she finally left that bastard."

Violet tensed in her chair and drank her coffee.

The men acknowledged they'd heard the news. "Wonder where she went?" one of them asked, an expression of boredom on his face. The other men shrugged.

Rita said, "I don't know, but I tell you, I wouldn't say even if I did know. That Billy's a mean son-of-a-bitch. He'd go after her and probably kill her this time."

Violet felt a wave of fear flush through her body. She sat like a rock, afraid to move.

Rita continued. "That Billy come in here looking for Rosie. Said she stole his money and took off. Butter wouldn't melt in his mouth when he was talking to me. Like I didn't know what kinda man he is. Son-of-a-bitch. As if he ever made a dime on his own, the lazy bum, living off of Rosie and her wages here."

Her mouth bleeding, Violet tried to reach the door. He pulled her back and smacked her face again. Hot tears stung her eyes and she couldn't see where the next blow was coming from, but she felt it, landing on her nose. A new flow of blood to add to the rest. "Lazy bitch. Can't even have my dinner ready when I get home. You know I like my dinner on time." The blows were coming from all directions now. How could one man have so many hands? The thought snapped across her mind as she struggled to get free. Don't fight him, he'll just get meaner. She tasted the blood in her mouth and bent over to retrieve her glasses. Broken. Again. A last kick to her butt. "I'll get your dinner."

Violet's hand trembled as she picked up her mug and drank the cooling liquid. Rita came over and poured more coffee. "You want anything to eat, honey? Our special is meat loaf sandwich, lots of gravy. I make the pies myself, so I know they're good." Rita's face was heavily made up: beige foundation, rose-colored rouge, blue eye shadow, black mascara, and red lipstick. Her face was kind and tired.

Violet wanted to leave but felt like she was welded to her chair. "I guess a piece of pie would be nice."

"Apple, cherry, pumpkin, strawberry, blueberry, or chocolate?"

"Cherry, please." Why did she always sound so meek? She cleared her throat. "I changed my mind. Apple."

"You're entitled," Rita said, as she went to get the pie. Bringing the slab of sugared crust leaking with fat slices of apples and cinnamon, Rita continued her tirade against Billy. "That man! Thought I never noticed Rosie's black eyes, her bruises. And that broken arm. Fell down the stairs, my foot! He probably pushed her. Twenty years married to that bum. Thank god, they didn't have any kids. I told her, I said, 'Rosie, you can't let him do that to you.' Said it so many times she must have got sick hearing me. More coffee, Cheryl?" Rita held up the pot and looked toward the woman eating the french fries.

"Yes, I could do with another cup." Cheryl's voice was soft. She glanced at Violet and smiled again. "You from around here?"

"I used to live near here. I'm just up visiting my grandma. I'm on my way home right now." Violet wanted to leave. She lurched from her chair and it made a loud scraping sound on the floor. The men turned to look at her. She fled to the washroom.

Broken arm. "I think my arm's broken. Please, I think you broke my arm." A kick to her stomach. "That right? Maybe I'll break the other one, bitch. You know I like starch in my shirts. Can't you do anything right?" The fist on her back, pounding on her back. Blows on her head. The arm dangling at her side, her useful one raised to stop the fists. Burning pain in her arm. She couldn't breathe from the pain. The fists pounding on her back, her shoulders. It stopped. "Get me a beer. Better go get that arm fixed. Dumb bitch." She'd get her arm fixed. Fell down the stairs. Again. How many times can you fall down the stairs before someone notices how accident-prone you are? Dumb bitch. She'd better think of a new excuse from now on.

Violet looked in the mirror of the washroom and rubbed her arm. He always called her dumb and ugly. She stared intently at the image in the mirror. Her new haircut took her by surprise. The short hair where there used to be a long, brown tangle. She adjusted the glasses on her nose. She wasn't ugly. Dumb maybe, for staying with him so long. She smiled at her reflection. I got away, didn't I?

She came out of the washroom and noticed that the men had left. She sat down to eat her pie. Cheryl was watching Rita clear the table where the men had been.

Rita stacked the dishes and carried them into the kitchen. She came out immediately. "I'll get to those later. Those old farts," she jerked her head to indicate the empty table. "They could care less about Rosie. Probably side with Billy. I tell you, men are all alike. Think a wife's there to get screwed and clean up their messes." She shook her head, the stiff red helmet of hair not moving an inch. "You married, hon?" she inquired of Violet.

"No."

"Smart girl. You get married and they just think they can boss you around to suit them. I guess you, me, and Cheryl's the only smart women left in this town. A couple of bachelorettes, that's us." Rita snorted and went back to the kitchen.

Violet finished her pie. She had wanted cherry, but the apple was good and filled the hollow space inside. From the kitchen came the sounds of dishes clattering and water being run. "Damn that Billy! Lost a waitress and I have to put up with him, sneaking around here and asking questions."

Cheryl said, "Rita's mad. Not about losing a waitress but about losing a friend. Rosie was a good woman."

"You act like she's dead," Violet said angrily. "More power to her, I say."

Cheryl looked surprised. "I know. I think the same as you. It takes guts to do what she did."

Guts. "I hate your guts, bitch." The slap in the face, the punch in the stomach. Her glasses flying off her face. "I don't know why you can't do anything right. Jesus Christ, this place is a pigsty. But that figures, a pig like you. Squaw. Can't even keep a man's house clean." She hurried to pick the newspapers off the floor and stacked them neatly on the table. "Come here." "No." "Come here!" Of course she went. His hands on her body, his mouth forcing hers open, his tongue pushing down her throat. "Bitch." As he raped her on the floor, her eyes wandered to the neat stack of newspapers sitting on the table. She looked at the table while he pushed and shoved inside her, her arms outflung at her sides. Finished. She lay on the floor, not sure of what he expected of her now. "Get me a beer."

"You O.K.?" Cheryl asked, concern on her face.

"Yeah. I was thinking of . . . nothing."

Rita came bustling out of the kitchen, carrying pies that she carefully set in the plastic covered containers by the coffee pot. Getting a rag, she began washing down the tables, checking the ketchup and mustard bottles, realigning the salt-and-pepper shakers. "Can I get you girls anything?"

Cheryl held up her mug to indicate more coffee.

Rita poured. "I tell you, I was just in the kitchen thinking about Rosie, wondering where she was. Do you think she went to one of them shelters? But how could she get there? And why didn't she call me? I would have driven her anywhere. Billy never let her drive his car, and she didn't have one. *His* car. As if her money didn't pay for it. God, I hate that man! Never could stand the sight of him. Strutting in here like some prize package. I never knew what she saw in him in the first place. Me and Rosie go way back together. Do you think she'll call me when she gets settled? You don't think she'll come back, do you? I'd sooner never see her again than think she might go back to that bastard." Rita's face was worried.

"No, I don't think she'll come back," Cheryl answered.

"Well, how do you know she won't? I remember one time she ran away and was staying with me. We had the best time together, then he comes crawling up to the door, begging her to come home. 'I didn't mean it,' he says, in that spineless voice of his. She looked at me like to say, what can I do? I know what she could have done. Stayed with me.

"Billy was afraid of me. Oh, he hated me, it was plain on his face, but he was scared of me just the same. She went back and he musta beat her real bad that time 'cause she called in to say she got the flu and wouldn't be in to work for a few days. I says to her, Rose Helen, I'm coming right over there to get you. But no, she wouldn't hear of it. I just got the flu, she says. So I let her be."

Rita wrung the cloth in her hands, the strong tendons standing out like ropes. "I'm glad she got away. Too bad she didn't shoot him and burn the house down, like that woman a few years back. Oh, Rosie." Her eyes became bright and wet, and she turned away and went into the kitchen.

She ran away, but she didn't have anywhere to go. She thought of calling Grandma, but Grandma didn't know the things he did to her and he might hurt Grandma if she took Violet in. She called in sick to work and took a bus to Traverse City. She wandered the streets, looking in shop windows, looking into people's faces. Nobody knew her here. Nobody knew what he did when the door was closed. Nobody knew. She pretended she was someone else. Just a woman going shopping, leisurely, taking her time, enjoying a day out. The freedom. The freedom of walking up the street. She was another person, not the dumb, ugly squaw he said she was. Even her body felt different. Like it belonged to her. *Her.* What would happen if she stayed here? She couldn't. She didn't have any money, only the clothes she was wearing, no place to stay. What was she thinking of? Not possible, not possible. She took the bus home. Of course he knew she had run away. She should have known he would find out. He cried this time. Promised he wouldn't hurt her anymore. Said he was scared she had left him for good. Promised he wouldn't hurt her anymore. She believed him. What else could she do, a dumb, ugly bitch like herself? Later that night he stomped on her feet and legs as if to punish the very limbs that dared to go walking, like a *real* person, up the street in Traverse City.

Violet looked up from the table. Cheryl was watching her, a look of sympathy in her lively brown eyes. "So you were visiting your grandma? Do you have other family here?"

"No. My mother died when I was twelve. My dad . . . I don't know where my dad is. I went to live with my grandma after Mom died. I haven't been back here for a while, about a year. My grandma's getting old, and I like to check on her, you know, see for myself how she's doing. I'd like her to come and live with me. She says she'll see, but I think that means no. She wouldn't like the city unless I could find a place that had a little grass or some trees. But I'm looking for a new place. Right now, I'm living in kind of a dump." Violet stopped. She could feel her cheeks getting hot. She never talked this much. "Are you from around here?" she asked Cheryl, anxious to get the conversation away from herself.

"No, I'm from Peshawbestown, the reservation past Traverse City. I'm just here for the summer, working in a place for women and children. We're starting something similar in my community, and I'm here to learn the ropes." Cheryl's full lips curved into a smile. "Naturally, our place will be more 'Indian style.' "

"My mother was from there."

"No kidding! What was her name? Maybe I know your family," Cheryl asked eagerly.

"I don't know her maiden name." What a stupid thing to say, Violet thought. What possible harm could come from telling Cheryl her mother's name? Was she going to live like this forever, afraid to tell people anything?

Rita hurried out of the kitchen. "Thought I heard the door. Must be going crazy! For a minute there, I thought it was Rosie. Didn't know whether to be mad or glad. You get my age, you start imagining things." She smiled weakly.

Cheryl said, "Your age indeed. You don't look a day over thirty-five."

Rita touched her hair. "Well, the dye job helps, don't it? Thirty-five, my foot! Thought I was the snow-job queen around here."

Cheryl and Rita laughed. Even Violet joined in, though her laugh was rusty and unused.

"I'll get you girls more coffee, then I think I'll join you and have a cigarette. Trying to quit," she said ruefully to Violet, "but it's only my second one today."

She brought the pot over and gestured to Violet. "Come on over here and sit with us."

Violet pulled out a chair and sat stiffly holding her coffee cup, pretending this was the most natural thing in the world for her to do-sit with women, share stories, share life.

"Well, this is nice," Rita took a deep drag from her cigarette and blew the smoke out gustily. "Just us girls. I can't get my mind off Rosie. Two days she's been gone and not a word. Not that I expect her to be rushing to a phone to call me. I expect this is the first time in her life she's had some breathing space. But I do want to hear from her.

"Ever since we was kids I've been worrying about her. Her dad was the biggest drunk in town. I know he used to beat Rosie's ma. I heard my own folks talking when they thought I wasn't listening. Rosie used to tell me things too. I won't repeat them. The woman's gotta have some dignity. It just got to be a natural thing. I'd think up ways to get Rosie out of that house, away from her dad. She slept over our house so much, my ma said she might as well adopt her. Oh, I prayed for that to happen, I did. We were like twins, never apart.

"And when we were teens, didn't that big, ugly Billy Claymore come into our lives and spoil everything. What she saw in him I just don't . . . well, I guess he was good to her for a while, made her think he'd take care of her. I saw right through him, but she wouldn't listen to me."

Rita puffed angrily at her cigarette and tapped the ashes into a metal tray. "She wouldn't listen to me. I was maid of honor at her wedding. Not much of a wedding, just standing in front of the justice of the peace. I helped her pick out her dress. It was pink and had a full skirt. We starched her crinolines so the dress stuck out real far. She looked so pretty. And happy. I'll guarantee that was the last happy day she had with that man. First and last!" She stubbed out her cigarette and lit a fresh one. "I cried. Told her I always cry at weddings. She would have believed anything on that day.

"She had on this cute little hat. White, with a veil that came down to her nose. She gave me that hat some years back. Said it just took up space in her closet. It looked like hell on me, but I kept it anyways. Girls, it's a terrible thing when you can't help a friend." She stubbed out her second cigarette with force.

"It sounds to me," Cheryl said, taking Rita's hand, "like you helped her all you could. You were a good friend to her. Most women don't have that."

"That's right," Violet blurted. "Women like that . . . we . . . they don't have any friends. Too scared or ashamed . . . or something." Her voice trailed away.

Rita squinted her eyes and gave Violet a long look. "You think she'll be O.K.?"

Her mother didn't have friends. "Just you and me, Violet. You're the best friend a mother ever needs." But she couldn't be the kind of friend her mom needed, the kind that would protect her from the jealous rampages of a husband. She was a little girl, not a grownup who could stand up to her father. And after her mom died from the cancer, he came to her and wanted to touch her, wanted to do things to her. What had she done to make him want to do things that only grownups are supposed to do? Was it because her body had matured so fast? She had started her period when she was eleven and her breasts got bigger and she started to grow hair under her arms and on her private place. *Private place.* That's what her mom used to call it. Was that why her dad wanted her to do things that she wasn't supposed to do? And then Grandma, her precious grandma, had come to take her to live with her. "You're not fit to raise this child," Grandma had told her father. "You're not fit." She had never told Grandma about the grown-up things dad had wanted her to do. Did she know? But if she'd known, would she have wanted Violet anyway? Violet never told, fearing the answer to the question she carried in her twelve-year-old heat. And it settled in her heart that it must have been her fault—her mother's beatings, her father's seductions—and she vowed to be a good girl from now on. Try to please everyone. Try very hard to please.

Cheryl was talking. "I bet she went to a shelter. They'll take good care of her there. She'll call you when she's got herself together, I'm sure of it."

"A while back I saw this TV show," Rita lit up another cigarette. "There was a woman on there from the shelter. She talked about women hating themselves and thinking they deserved the beatings they was getting. I thought, that's my Rose Helen. No matter how many times I told her she was worth something, that she was a wonderful woman, *she* didn't believe it, so why would she believe me? At the end of the show they gave some numbers to call. I copied them down and gave them to Rosie. What's this? she said. I told her they was phone numbers for women shelters. A woman could go there and get away from her husband and they'd keep her safe. She gave me a look, I tell you, I don't ever want to see that look again. Like a whipped dog. Like she was ashamed 'cause her own husband was beating on her. Like it was all her fault! I tell you, girls, I like to die to see that look on my Rose Helen's face." Rita's mascara was running in dark rivers down her face, and she lifted a hand to wipe away the black smudges. Violet handed her a napkin, the smiling turkeys a malicious joke against Rita's pain-filled face as she wiped her eyes. "I'm not a praying woman, but I pray that Rosie's safe and learning how to love herself. Like I love her."

Love yourself. Her counselor had brought that incredibly unthinkable idea to Violet. It took her days to sort through the thoughts that were making a mess in her brain. Wasn't it enough that she had found strength to leave her husband? Finally making that call to the shelter, to her grandma, who had saved her once and now had to do it again. Must she think about loving herself? A dumb, ugly bitch? A squaw? A pig? A woman who couldn't make dinner on time, starch his shirts right, pick up newspapers that she dared to read and leave lying on the floor? Her self? Love? Slowly, so slowly, she started to put the little scraps together, the bits of herself that she could love. Like piecing together a quilt, she basted the parts in her mind with fragile thread. It wasn't finished yet, but someday the cloth would be whole and she would cover herself with the multicolored blocks.

"My mother's name was Johnson." Violet looked at Cheryl and smiled.

"I know so many Johnsons, it'll take us forever to figure it out," Cheryl laughed, touching Violet's hand delicately with her own.

Violet reached for her coffee and relaxed in her chair. Cheryl gave her hand a last pat and asked, "You ever gone back to where your mom came from?"

"No, but I've thought about it. You know, just to see where she lived when she was a girl. She used to talk about it, and so did my grandma. They moved from therer when my mom was just a kid. Maybe the next time I come here, I'll drive up that way and take Grandma too."

"You do that, honey," Rita piped in. "And when you do, be sure to stop by here and see me." She blew her nose and got up, gathering the ashtray and coffee mug. "Just help yourself to more coffee, girls. I'll be in the kitchen doing up the dishes. Maybe I'll put together more pies. Supper crowd's gonna be coming in soon." She made her way to the kitchen, turning to smile at Cheryl and Violet. "You girls sure were a blessing to me today. I just know Rosie's gonna be O.K. I feel it somehow. And I'll be there for her, like I always been." Rita smiled again, her face transformed into that of a young woman. She went through the kitchen door, her red hair blazing like a flag.

"I guess I better get going," Violet said. "I'm starting a new job tomorrow and there's a million things I need to do, plus two more hours of driving ahead of me."

"Good luck with your new job. You know, Rosie's O.K. She's at the shelter where I work. I can't tell Rita, but I think I wanted to come in here today just to reassure her." Cheryl looked sad. "I didn't know Rita loved her so much."

"I'm glad I met you, Cheryl. Maybe we'll see each other again."

"Well, just to make sure, here's my name and address. I'll be home in October. You bring your grandma, and we'll track down those people of yours." She dug in her purse and wrote down the information on a slip of paper. "I hope you come. Everyone should know where they're from, where home is." She handed Violet the paper, their hands touching briefly.

Violet got out her wallet and left a five-dollar bill on the table. "I'll be back. Thank you, Cheryl."

"For what?"

"Oh, caring about Rita and Rosie. Everything." Violet slung her purse over her shoulder. "Tell Rita good-bye for me. Tell her. . .tell her that it might take a long time, but Rosie will make it." She smiled into Cheryl's face.

She walked out of the diner and got in her car. Turning on the ignition, Violet looked once again at the sign of the wild turkey.

"Sometimes we fly real high."

This Place

"Mother, I am gay. I have AIDS." The telephone call that it almost killed him to make.

The silence. Then, "Come home to us."

David came home because he was dying. He expected to see his place of birth in a new way, as if he were a photographer capturing scenes through diverse lenses. *Scene one: through a living man's eyes. Scene Two: through a dying man's eyes.* But the beauty remembered was the beauty that still existed. Nothing had changed in ten years. The water of the Bay just as blue and smooth. The white pines just as tall and green. The dirt roads as brown and rutted as the day he had left. His mother as small and beautiful, her dark hair with even more grey streaks running through the braid she wrapped around her head.

Had nothing changed but him?

He had left this place and gone to the city to look for other men like himself. He found them. He found a new life, a different life. He found so much. Even the virus that now ate at him. David came home and was afraid of death.

David could feel the virus changing his body, making marks on his insides. Outside, too, his body was marked: by the tumors growing on his face and the paleness of his skin. He worried that the virus was somehow taking away his color, bleaching the melanin that turned him polished copper in the summer and left him light terra cotta in winter. He could feel the virus at way with the melanin and he could not check the battle. He couldn't hold this virus in his fist and squeeze the death out of it. He could only wait and look in the mirror to see the casualty of this war. David was afraid.

"Mother, am I turning white?"

"No, my baby son. You are dark and beautiful. Your hair is black and shiny as ever. Your eyes are tired, but still as brown and strong as the day you left this place."

He knew she lied to him. Mothers lie about their children's pain. *It will go away, they say. I'll make it better, they say. Oh, Mother, make it better, make it go away. I'm afraid of death.*

He felt the virus eating his hair. It fell out in clumps as he combed it. His forehead got broader and receded further. The blackness of the strands had dulled to some nondescript color. His braid was thin and lifeless, not as it used to be, snapping like a whip across his back, or gliding down his back like a snake.

David's sister brought her children to see him. They crawled on his lap and kissed him. He as afraid for them. Afraid the virus would reach out of his body and grab these babies and eat at them until they, too, disappeared in its grip. The virus put a fear in him—a fear that he could wipe out his people by breathing, by talking, by living. David saw, in his dreams, the virus eating away at this place until it was gone.

His dreams were also about a place called death. Death seemed to be a gaping hole in the world where David looked and there was nothing. He would wake from these dreams sweating, his limbs filled with pain. He had lived his life so well, so hard, clutching it to him like food, swallowing and being nourished. He wanted to greet death like that, opening his arms to it, laughing and embracing that other world. But he was afraid.

"Mother, I am afraid of death."

"Joseph is coming to visit."

On a day when David was seated in his chair before the window, looking out at the way the bright sun had turned everything in the yard golden, he heard the pickup truck making its way down the dirt road to the house. He also heard a voice singing. David laughed out loud. The song being sung was "All My Exes Live in Texas," and he knew that Joseph was on his way to him.

The truck came to a screeching, convulsive stop. David's mother went out to greet the man who jumped from the truck laughing, "Where's the patient?" As David watched, Joseph extracted a brown paper bag and an orange-striped cat from the truck. "Meet my friend, the Prophet. You can call her Prophet." David's mother reached for the cat who nudged at her breast and looked into her face. Joseph kissed Grace on the cheek. Prophet licked Grace's face. David wondered at the fact that Joseph looked the same as he had when David was a child. Dressed in faded jeans and a flannel shirt, Joseph's face was lean and unlined. His nose was sharp and slightly curved at the end, like a bird's beak.

His eyes were black and round, reminding David again of a bird, perhaps a kestrel or a falcon. Joseph wore long, beaded earrings that draped across the front of his shirt. His hair, black and coarse, was tied back with a leather string. His fingers were covered with silver-and-garnet studded rings, his hands delicate but used. Joseph looked at the young man in the window and lifted his hand in a greeting. Then he smiled and his face took on the unfinished look of a child. David waved back, feeling excitement—the way he used to feel before going to a party.

"This ain't goin' to be like any party you ever went to," Joseph remarked as he stepped through the doorway. "Here, have a Prophet," and he lifted the orange cat from Grace's arms onto David's lap.

Prophet looked intently at David's face, then kneaded his lap and settled herself on it, where she purred. David stroked the orange fur and scratched the cat's head. She burrowed deeper in his lap. "I would get up to greet you, but I think Prophet's got something else in mind."

Joseph laughed. "We wouldn't want to disturb her highness. David, we have not seen each other in many years." He bent down to kiss the young man on his forehead. "You don't look so good." Joseph eyed him critically.

"Thanks. But you look the same as ever."

"You in a lot of pain," Joseph said in a statement, not a question.

"Yeah, a lot of pain. I take about fifty pills a day. They don't seem to make that much of a difference." David continued to stroke Prophet.

"You think I can cure you?"

"No."

"Good, because I can't. All of us are afraid of death, though. We don't know what to expect, what to take with us." He looked in his paper sack. "Maybe I got the right things here."

Grace went into the kitchen, and Joseph pulled up a chair and sat beside David. Looking at Prophet asleep on David's lap, Joseph remarked, "Cats is smart. This one had a brother looked just like her. I called him Tecumseh. One morning I woke up and he was gone. I asked the Prophet if she knew where her brother went. She looked at me and blinked, then turned her head away like I'd

85

said somethin' rude. I went outside to look for Tecumseh and I found him, layin' dead under a rose bush. It was a good year for the roses, they was bloomin' to beat the band. He had chosen the red roses to die under. That was a good choice, don't you think? I buried him under that red rose bush. The old man knew what *he* wanted, but he had to let me know, me not bein' as smart as a cat. Prophet came out and sat on the grave. She sat there for three days and nights. Cats are different from us. We worry about fittin' things to our own purpose. Cats don't worry about them things. They live, they die. They get buried under a red rose bush. Smart, huh?"

"You got any spare rose bushes? Only make mine flaming pink!" David laughed, then began coughing, blood spattering the Kleenex he held to his mouth.

The Prophet jumped from David's lap and sat on the floor, her back to him.

"Now I've done it," David gasped, "Come back. Here kitty, kitty, kitty."

The Prophet turned and gave him a look of contempt, her back twitching, her tail moving back and forth on the floor.

"Huh," Joseph said. "She ain't comin' back for a while. Don't like the name Kitty."

Grace came in to announce dinner. David grabbed his cane and shuffled to the table. He sat down, gasping for breath. "Takes longer every time. I think I'm losing feeling in my right leg, but what the hell, I'd crawl to the table for Mother's beef stew." He half-heartedly lifted the spoon to his mouth. "My appetite's still pretty good, isn't it, Mother?"

Grace smiled at her son. "The day your appetite goes is the day I go."

She had made fresh bread to eat with the stew and set dishes of pickles and cheese on the table. Joseph rubbed his hands together in glee. "This looks good!" They ate, talking local gossip, the Prophet sitting daintily beside Joseph's chair. David's hands shook as he barely fed himself, spilling stew on his blue shirt. Grace fussed and tied a napkin around his neck. David smiled, "Next, she'll be feeding me or giving me a bottle." He winked at his mother and blew a kiss across the table to her. She caught it and put it on her cheek.

Joseph watched while he fed bits of meat to Prophet. He looked in his sack and pulled out a dish covered in waxed paper. "I made these this mornin'. Butter tarts. The flakiest crust you'll find anywhere. You gotta use lard, none of of that shortenin'. Lard is what makes a crust that'll melt in your mouth. It's my gift to you, David."

As David bit into the sweetness of the tart, he looked at Joseph, his earrings swinging against his shoulders, his hands making patterns in the air as he described the making of the tarts, and David thought, *He acts like a queen.* He looked harder at Joseph, thinking, if you put him in a city, in a gay bar, the old nelly really would fit right in. David laughed out loud.

Grace looked startled, but Joseph grinned and nodded his head. "Catchin' on, my young friend?"

As he helped clear the table, David smiled with his new knowledge. Collapsing into his reclining chair, David swallowed his medicine and laid his head back, closing his eyes. He could hear the murmurs between Joseph and Grace, his mother always a living, vivid presence in his life-his reason for hanging on so long to life. "I love you, Mother." he whispered. He opened his eyes to the dry touch of Joseph's fingers on his face. His mother was bringing out the moccasins she had made from rabbit hide and had beaded the nights they sat and watched TV. She presented them to Joseph. He unlaced his red hightops and slipped the beautiful moccasins on his feet. He put his feet out in front of him in admiration. He got up and walked in the,. He jumped and clicked his heels together. "Thank you, Grace. You haven't lost your touch, have you? Now it's time for you to go. Don't come back till the mornin'."

Grace gathered her things together and stood looking at David. Her face shifted with emotions: sorrow, pride, fear, love. She kissed her son and hugged Joseph. They watched her leave.

Joseph turned and asked David, "You tryin' to be brave for your mom? Let me tell you somethin' about mothers. They know everything. She feels what you're goin' through. Can't hide it, even though you try."

"No! I don't want her to know how bad it gets. I can see it in her face, she gets crazy not knowing what to do for me. But this is the real crazy part, I don't want to let go of her. That death. . .that place. . .she won't be there."

The Prophet jumped on Joseph's lap and began washing herself. "That's true. Her time isn't here yet. David, you have lived your life in the way that was best for you. You think Grace didn't know why you left here? Think she didn't know you was gay? You can't tell someone like Grace not to go crazy when her son is dyin'. You can't tell her how to mourn you. And you can't be draggin' her along with you when you leave this place."

"I don't want to do that. I feel like a little kid when I was scared of a nightmare. Mother would make it go away. Death is like that nightmare. I gotta meet it on my own, but I'm scared."

"Yes, I know you are," and Joseph reached for David's hand. David's bony fingers closed over Joseph's.

"When I lived in the city, I used to get so homesick for this place. I'd picture the way it looked—the sky, the trees, my relatives. I'd dream it all up in my mind, but I never thought I would come back. I made my life in the city, thinking that I couldn't come back here. My people don't want queers, faggots living among them. But now, some of us are coming home to die. Where else would we go but back to our homes, our families? What a joke, eh? They couldn't deal with my life, now they gotta deal with my death. God, I think about the guys that really can't go home. They have to die alone in some hospital, or even on the street. There was guy I knew, Ojibwe, and he died outside his apartment. I heard about it after it happened and I got in this rage! People just walking by him, probably thinking, oh here's another drunk Indian, just walking by him! And him, getting cold and no one would touch him." Tears were moving down David's face. He lifted his hand to wipe his face. "That's when I hated being an Indian. My own people, hateful to that guy. He was scared to go home. Probably thought they'd throw him out again, or stone him or something."

"Well, Indians got no immunity from hatefulness or stupidity, David. Maybe he had made his choice to die alone. Maybe he didn't have a home to go to."

David looked shocked. "No, that can't be true. I know what it's like. I grew up here, remember? It seemed like I had to make a choice, be gay or be an Indian. Some choice, eh? So I moved to the city." David sighed, then began to cough.

Joseph stroked Prophet, whose ears were twitching. "Even a city can't take the Indian part away. Even a virus can't do that, my young friend." He dipped into his sack and held out a piece of metal to David. "Look in this. What do you see?"

David held the piece of metal to his face. He saw a blurred image of himself, tumors covering his face. When he tilted the piece of tin, he saw himself laughing and dressed in his finest clothes, dancing in the bar in the city. He tilted it yet another way and saw himself dancing at a pow wow, his hair fanning out as he twirled and jumped. In another tilt, he saw himself as a child, sitting on Grandmother's lap.

"Which one is you?" Joseph asked.

"All of them."

"When the Prophet was a kitten," Joseph said, petting the now sleeping cat, "she used to keep me awake at night. She'd jump on my head just as I was dozin' off. I'd knock her away and turn over, but just when that sweet moment of sleep was callin' me, she'd jump on my head again. I thought maybe she was hungry and I'd get up to feed her. She'd eat, then start the whole routine all over again. She even got Tecumseh in the act. While she'd jump on my head, he'd get under the covers and bite my feet. I finally gave up and got out of bed and went outside and looked at the sky. About the fifth night of these carryin' ons, I *really* looked at the sky. I saw all the stars as if they was printed on the insides of my eyes. I saw the moon like she really was. And I started to pray to Sky Woman, blinkin' and shinin' up there. She answered me back, too, all because the cats was smarter than me. Nothin' hides in front of old Sky Woman. You might think she's hidin' when you can't see her, but she's there, checkin' everything out. People can't hide from her. And people can't hide from themselves."

"Is that what I've done?" David asked, his face sad. "I've always been proud of being Mohawk, of being from here. I *am* proud of being gay even though everywhere I turned, someone was telling me not to be either. In the city they didn't want me to be Native. In this place, they don't want me to be gay. It can drive you crazy!

Be this. Be that. Don't be this way. So you get to be like an actor, changing roles and faces to please somebody out there who hates your guts for what you are." David laughed. "When I was diagnosed I thought, well, now I don't have to pretend anymore. It's all out in the open. I'm going to die, and why did I waste my time and tears worrying about all this other stuff? I got real active in AIDS work. I wanted to reach out to all the Indian gays I knew, form support groups, lean on each other. 'Cause the other guys just didn't understand us. I was a fireball for two years, real busy, but then I got too sick to do much of anything. My friends were good, but they couldn't take care of me anymore. I came home. Here I sit, Grandfather, waiting for death, but scared shitless."

Joseph began to hum and sing, "Crazy. . . I'm crazy for feelin' so lonely." He stuck his hand inside the sack and handed David a piece of paper.

We, as the original inhabitants of this country, and sovereigns of the soil, look upon ourselves as equally independent and free as any other nation or nations. This country was given to us by the Great Spirit above; we wish to enjoy it, and have our passage along the lake, within the line we have pointed out. The great exertions we have made, for this number of years, to accomplish a peace and have not been able to obtain it; our patience, as we have observed, is exhausted. We, therefore, throw ourselves under the protection of the Great Spirit above, who will order all things for the best. We have told you our patience is worn out, but that we wish for peace and whenever we hear that pleasing sound, we shall pay attention to it. Until then, you will pay attention to us.

"My ancestor. Quite a man." David held the paper in his thin hands.

"Yes, he was. Diplomats, they called him and his sister. We call them warriors."

David read the words again. "Grandfather, I would like to be a warrior like this man. I would like to see death coming and run to meet it, not afraid, not hiding behind my mother."

"Who says you ain't a warrior? David, the bravest people I knew were the ones that lived and kept on livin'. Those two, Tyendinaga and Molly, they fought to keep us alive as a people. Looks to me like you're as fine a warrior as they was. David, you lived!"

The Prophet suddenly came awake and stretched to her full length. She sat up and washed her face. She blinked at David, her yellow eyes staring at him until he looked away. She jumped off Joseph's lap and settled herself in front of David's feet.

"Trust the Prophet to interrupt the proceedings. Let's go outside and sit on the porch." Joseph stood up and stretched his arms and shook his legs.

David reached for his cane, his body curved and stooped. Joseph got a blanket to wrap him in against the cool night air. David made his way toward the front door. Joseph went to the kitchen and brought out two mugs of coffee and the rest of the butter tarts. They settled on the porch steps.

"David, look at the moon. When she's a crescent like that, I think Sky Woman's smilin' at us. More than likely, laughin'. She has big jobs to do like pullin' in the tides, and we sit here yappin' about life and death."

"The moon is beautiful. Somehow, it never seemed to shine like that in the city." David began coughing again, his body shaking throbbing.

Joseph held onto him until the shaking stopped. "David, you're just a rez boy, ain't you? Nothin' looks as good as here, eh? But I think so too. One time, a long time ago, I thought about leavin' here."

"Why didn't you? It can't have been easy for you. Or were things different then? Maybe not so homophobic, not so much hatred?"

"Oh, things was bad. But not in that way. There was hatred, alright. The kind that makes people turn to the bottle or put a gun in their mouth and shoot." David winced, remembering his father's death. Joseph continued. "That kind of hatred, self-hatred. I stayed because I was supposed to. I fought it, but I had to stay. It was my job." He began a song. "*Your cheatin' heart will tell on you. You'll cry and cry, the way I do.* Sing with me, David." And they sang until the last words were finished and Joseph hugged David.

"I thought medicine men were supposed to chant and cast spells, not sing old Hank Williams' songs," David teased.

Joseph looked surprised. "Oh, some do. Some do. But how many medicine people you know, David?"

"Only you, Grandfather."

"Well then, there you go. What you see is what you get."

"When my father died, I remember being shut out from what was going on. I know they were all trying to protect me and Sister, but we were scared. One day he was there, the next day he wasn't. He wasn't the greatest dad, but he was ours! You were there, Grandfather. Why did he do it?"

Joseph took a deep breath and let it out. It lingered in the night air like a puff of smoke. "Because he didn't know any other way. Are you judgin' him, David? 'Cause if you are, you can forget it. Too many people made a judgment on your father all his life. He doesn't need yours to add to it." Joseph's face became angry, then softened as he took David's hand again. "Children get scared. We fail you because we fail ourselves. We think *you'll* get over it because you're younger and have fewer memories. Grownups are fools, David. Your father didn't know what else to do with his life, a life he thought was worthless. So he shot it away."

David wept. "I've thought about shooting mine away, like him. Like father, like son, isn't that what the people would say? So, I didn't, all because I didn't want to be mentioned in the same breath with him. Pride, that's all that kept me going. And I couldn't do the same thing to my mother and sister that he did to us."

"You're a lot like your dad. Sweet, like he was. Oh yes," Joseph looked at David's disbelieving face, "a sweet man. When we was at residential school together, he's the one that took me under his wing. He fought the grownups and the other kids that ganged up on me. He was always my friend. He didn't fail me, ever. And I tried not to let him down, but I wasn't enough to keep that gun out of his hand. Nobody was enough, David. Not you, or your mom or your sister. Don't you judge him. He wouldn't have judged you." Joseph raised his face to the crescent moon and closed his eyes.

David felt a small piece of pain dislodge from inside him. It floated away in the night's darkness. "Thank you for telling me that, Grandfather. I always loved him."

Joseph smiled, his crooked teeth shining white in the moon's light. "Love is a funny thing, David. It stays constant, like her," he pointed to the crescent. "When you cut through all the crap, the need and greed part, you got the good, lastin' stuff. She knew that," and he pointed again to the moon. "She put herself up there to remind us of her love, not to admire her pretty shine. Of course, the pretty shine doesn't hurt, does it?" And they laughed together.

David said, "I met my pretty shine in the city. He will always be the love of my life, even though he doesn't feel that way about me. We're still friends. . . God, the city was so different for me—I loved it! Excitement. All those gorgeous men. If I'd stayed here, I wouldn't have known the world was full of gay people. If I'd stayed here though, maybe I wouldn't have gotten AIDS." David pulled the blanket closer around himself and shivered.

Joseph squeezed David's wasting fingers. "Do you regret any of it?"

"No. I've thought about that a lot. I only wish I could have stayed, but I thought I had to make the choice and don't know what would have happened if I hadn't left."

Joseph rustled in his sack. "Who can read the future? Well, maybe I can, but can you read the past as well? Here, take this."

David held out his hand. A dry snakeskin was deposited into his dry palm. The skin was faded but still showed orange-and-black markings.

"I saw this snake shed her skin. I was walking in the bush and heard a very small noise. I watched her wriggle out of her old life, just like she was removin' an overcoat. It took this snake a long time, but then, there she was in her new overcoat, her old skin just lyin' there waitin' for me to pick it up and give it to you."

"Thank you, Grandfather. It's beautiful." David touched the snakeskin and looked into Joseph's face. "I think it would be wonderful if we could shed ourselves like this and have a brand-new beautiful skin to face the world. Or maybe, to face death."

"We do, David. A snake doesn't put on a new skin with different colors. She has the same one, just layers of it. She doesn't become a new snake, but older and wiser with each shedding. Humans shed. We don't pay attention to it, thought. We get new chances all the time. A snake makes use of her chances; that's why she's a snake and we're not. We never know when we got a good thing going'."

"That's true! Mother used to tell me I was lucky. I had it good compared to other little boys. She was right, of course." David giggled into his hand. "She is always right. Why is that, Grandfather?"

"Now you got me. That's something I'll never know either!"

They laughed, the sound filling the night air. Prophet scratched at the door to be let out. "The Prophet's afraid she's missin' out on something. Those butter tarts, maybe." Joseph got up to open the door.

The Prophet streaked out the open door and ran to the cluster of apple trees. She climbed one and sat on a branch. David could see the yellow glow of her eyes as she watched the men drink their coffee and bite into the tarts.

Joseph remarked between bites, "Prophet does it every time. I'd sit around all night talkin' if she didn't remind me why I was here."

David started to shake. "I'm afraid, Grandfather."

"Yes, I know, David. We'll go inside, and you can lay down while I make some special tea. I'm here with you, David. I won't leave you."

David clutched the snakeskin in his hand and struggled to his feet. He made his way into the house and to the couch where he started coughing and spitting up blood. Joseph cleaned David's face and wrapped the blanket tightly around his skinny body. He went to the kitchen, and David could hear him singing, "I fall to pieces . . . each time I see you again." David smiled, the voice reassuring to him.

"The Prophet's still in that apple tree, starin' at the house," said Joseph, as he brought a steaming mug of liquid to David.

David sipped the tea and made a face. "What is this stuff? It tastes like wet leaves!"

"It is wet leaves. Drink up. It's good for what ails you."

"Yeah, right," David smiled, "I notice you're not drinking any."

"Well, I'm not the sick one, am I?"

David drank the brew, watching Joseph walk around the room, picking up books and stacking them neatly, straightening a picture hanging on the wall, tidying a lamp table. "There's a dust rag in the broom closet. The rug could use a shake and the windows need a wash," David said teasingly.

"You're a regular Henny Youngman, ain't you?"

"Who?"

"All finished?" Joseph pointed to the mug. "If you want more, you can't have it. I only brought enough for one cup."

David pushed the mug toward Joseph. "Please, no more. I think I'll survive without it."

"Ah, survival. Let me tell you about that one." Joseph sat on the couch at David's feet.

David felt heavy in his body. He tried to lift his hand, but it was too much of an effort. He tried to speak, but his voice wouldn't move out of him. He looked at Joseph who was talking, but his voice was thin and far away. He saw that Prophet had come back into the house and was sitting on Joseph's lap. The Prophet stared at David with her yellow eyes and smiled at him. Was that a smile? What was that tea? Wet leaves . . . and David was falling was falling back into wet leaves and it was autumn the air smelled like winter he was a boy a boy who jumped up from wet leaves and ran he ran he was chasing something he felt so good so good this is what childhood is you run you laugh you open your mouth you feel the wind on your tongue the sun on your head the apple trees were giving up their gifts of fruit you picked an apple you feel you taste the juice running down your throat the apple made a loud crunch as you bit and the swallows in the tree were waiting for the core to be thrown down so they could share the fruit of the tree the geese were flying you ran you ran into the cornfield and scared the pheasant who was picking at the seed you laughed you laughed it was a perfect day you picked up a feather and put it in your pocket the day was perfect when you were a child you ran you laughed you played you were loved you loved you were a child it was good so good good to be a child in this place this place this place never changed this place this place.

David opened his eyes. The Prophet was washing her tail. Joseph held a turtle rattle in his left hand. He was talking . . . *and then the church people sent their missionaries here to teach us to be Christian but we. . .*

David was falling he fell into the sound of the turtle's rattle he fell into the turtle's mouth he shook his body shook and . . . *fought them* . . . he fell into the sound of the rattle he was the rattle's sound the music the music he was dancing dancing with the first man he ever loved they were dancing holding holding the music the music the turtle's music was in them through them in them . . . *killed us* . . . he went home he went with the first man he ever loved the music was beating was beating their hearts the rattle the music they fell onto the bed the music the music touched them the turtle touched them the rattle touched them they touched they touched the touching was music was music his body singing music his body the rattle of the turtle the first man he loved . . . *we fought back*. . . their bodies singing shaking joining joining everything was music was music so good so good good the first man he loved Thomas Thomas . . . *they kept killing us off* . . . Tommy Tommy singing sighing joining . . . *but we* . . singing our bodies singing Tommy David Tommy Tommy . . . *survived* . . . .

David's eyes opened. The room was dark. The Prophet was staring, smiling, her eyes brilliant yellow. Joseph was staring also, his eyes sending out shafts of brilliance, laser beams into his soul.

"Grandfather."

Joseph held up the rattle and sang a song with no words, a song in a high, quivering voice. Joseph's face changed shape. He became a cat. The Prophet sat smiling, her teeth white in the dark room. Joseph sang and he became a snake hissing his song, his eyes sending out shards of light. Joseph sang and shook the turtle. He sang.

"Grandfather."

David was falling he fell into the song of the cat the song of the wolf the song of the snake the song of the turtle he fell he fell into the turtle's mouth the turtle's song he was shaking was shaking his grandmother was singing was singing a song a song in Indian his grandmother was singing singing he was singing with Grandmother he was sitting on Grandma's lap her lap she was holding him close so close . . . *our people survived* . . . she sang his mother sang his sister sang his father sang he sang he was singing in Indian Indian the voices the songs in Indian . . . *the sicknesses came* . . . singing singing his grandmother holding him his mother his father singing . . . *measles, smallpox* . . . Grandmother talking singing in Indian the language the song of Indian the people the song Grandma's hair brushing against his face as she whispered and told him he . . . *AIDS* . . . was an Indian Indian Mohawk singing songs Mohawk the voices Kanienka 'ha'ka the song the song of this place this Indian place this place.

The rattle was silent. The Prophet was sitting in a hump, the fur around her neck electric, like an orange ruff. Joseph sat, his laser eyes bright in the face of an old, old man. He spoke his voice not audible, the words not recognizable, and David heard.

"They took parts of us and cut them up and threw them to the winds. They made lies we would believe. We look for the parts to put ourselves back together. To put the earth back together, it is broken. We look for truth to put us all together again. There is a piece here. A part there. We scavenge and collect. Some pieces are lost. We will find them. Some parts are found, and we do not see them yet. We gather the pieces and bring them together. *We* bring them together. *We* make the truth about ourselves. *We* make the truth."

David was falling was falling he fell he fell into the sound of the ancient voice the ancient words he was falling into the sounds of screaming screaming in his face dirty Indian faggot fucking fact the voices screaming you dirty Indian you the sound of fists of fists the sound of hate the sound of hate you dirty Indian you dirty faggot the sound of hate the sound of blood the taste of blood in his mouth the taste the hate the hate . . . *we collect the parts that have been damaged* . . . the hate the pain as they raped you dirty Indian faggot the hate the blood the rape the sound of rape . . . *we hunt for the pieces* . . . the hate the pain the fear the dirty Indian faggot . . . *we gather it all together* . . . you filthy Indian scum you dirty you dirty you dirty . . . *we are the resisters, warriors* . . . you dirty Indian you dirty faggot the rape the sound of you dirty filthy . . . *we do not believe the lies they* . . . the taste the taste the taste of hate in his mouth.

David cried out. Joseph stroked his thinning hair, the turtle held over his body. "They hurt us in so many ways. The least of what they did was to kill us. They turned us into missing parts. Until we find those missing parts we kill ourselves with shame, with fear, with hate. All those parts just waitin' to be gathered together to make us. Us. A whole people. The biggest missing piece is love, David. *Love!*"

The Prophet leapt in the air and hissed. She leapt again and knocked the turtle rattle back into Joseph's lap.

"The Prophet says we are not finished. Who am *I* to argue with *her?*"

David tugged at the man's arm. "Joseph. Grandfather. I am so thirsty, so thirsty."

David was falling was falling into the shake of the rattle he fell he fell into the turtle's mouth he fell he was flying he flew he was inside the turtle the turtle shook he fell into voices voices asking him are you ready his heart his heart was beating are you ready his heart grew larger his heart was beating his heart was beating his heart the turtle asked him are you ready his grandmother held out her hand and touched him are you ready are you ready his grandmother touched his heart are you ready his father touched his heart are you ready the people held out their hands are you ready he reached for their hands his heart was beating inside the turtle a drum a drum are you ready Turtle touched his heart are you ready he fell he put out his arms he held out his arms I am ready they touched him I am ready I am ready I am ready.

David opened his eyes. The taste of tears was in his mouth. "I saw it." Prophet jumped delicately on David's chest and licked the salt tears from his face. She sat back on her haunches and watched David speak. "I saw my grandmother, my father. They touched me." He began coughing again, retching blood.

Joseph held a towel to David's mouth and touched the young man's face. "You found your parts, your pieces." Digging into his sack, he pulled out a white feather. "This is from a whistling swan. They stop here in the spring before goin' on to Alaska. The thing about them-they never know what they'll find when they get there. They just know they got to get there. When our bodies are no longer here, *we* are still here." He stood up, his joints creaking and snapping. "Your mother is comin'. The sun is real bright today. It's a good day to go." He scooped Prophet up from David's lap and draped her across his shoulder.

"Thank you, Grandfather," David whispered, his breath coming in ragged bursts.

David heard him go out the front door. He couldn't see, but he heard Joseph talking to the Prophet. He heard the truck door slam and the engine start its rattling and wheezing. David moved his hands on the blanket to find the tin, the snakeskin, his ancestor's words, the feather. He touched them and felt Joseph's presence. The sound of his mother's car made him struggle to sit up. He heard the door open and the footsteps of his mother coming into the room. He felt her standing by him, her cool fingers touching his face and hands.

He opened his mouth to say good-bye.

Food & Spirits

for my Dad

Elijah Powless decided it was time to take a trip.

He was driven to the bus stop by his son and daughter-in-law who, at the last moment, asked again, "Are you sure you want to do this, Father?"

And for the tenth or twentieth time he answered, "I want to see my granddaughters in the city. They are women now, and before I die I want to see how they are doin'."

Daughter-in-law shook her head but refrained from saying the usual: "You're not going to die. You see the girls all the time when they come to visit." She just shook her head, worried about letting an eighty-year-old man ride on a bus for seven hours to go to a place he'd never been. A big city. A big city in the States. A big city with the reputation of being the murder capital of the world!

Elijah had no faith in what newspapers or TV knew about a city. His twin granddaughters lived there-that was enough for him to go on.

The twins, Alice and Annie, were thrilled but anxious about their grandfather's trip. They offered to pay for the train fare and had even investigated plane routes and prices, but Elijah was firm in his insistence on paying for the bus ride himself.

"I'll see more from a bus. It's October, it'll be real pretty to see the land from a bus window. Besides, I don't want the twins to put out their hard-earned money on my trip."

So the daughter-in-law and the son had dutifully packed the suitcase and said many prayers. Elijah had also determined that he would take a bag of whitefish, frozen and wrapped in newspaper, and a separate bag of fry bread because, as Elijah said, "They don't get this kind of food in Detroit. I'll just make sure they have enough to last a few days."

"Please be careful, Father," the daughter-in-law breathed in his ear as she hugged him good-bye.

Elijah promised to be careful, though he wondered what he would have to be careful of. He had lived a good life. He had survived the Great Depression with a wife and five children. He had nursed his wife through cancer and on to death. He'd lost two sons to the white world and the alcohol in it. His three remaining children had finished school, had gotten jobs. The son standing before him now was a carpenter in a union, had a good wife, had twin daughters who were a joy in Elijah's life. He had been sad when the twins moved to the States to work for the Indian Center there. He was surprised that they had left home, but the twins were surprising girls. They were women now, he reminded himself. Thirty years old, unmarried, and Annie had declared she was thinking about adopting a child. It would be nice, Elijah thought, to be a great-grandfather to Annie's child. That was partly the reason he was taking this trip. He had it in mind that those Natives down there would listen to a man like himself. In fact, he was sure of it.

Getting on the bus and finding a seat, he waved good-bye to his son and daughter-in-law. He remarked to the woman sitting next to him, "My children are unhappy that I'm taking a trip. They think I'm too old and I need to be careful."

The woman turned her wide, fresh face toward him and smiled. Her false teeth glowed. "These kids sure do like to worry, don't they? They can't imagine that we old-timers might want to have some fun too." She whispered to Elijah, "I'm going to Windsor to visit my boyfriend. My daughter is scandalized that a woman my age has a beau."

Elijah was scandalized too. "You are a handsome woman. How come you only got one?"

They were laughing as the bus pulled out of the terminal. Well, this is good, Elijah told himself. A good sign. Laughter at the beginning means laughter at the end.

Elijah was trying to figure out how the woman got her hair that shade of blue when she stuck out her hand. "My name is Shirley Abbott."

"Elijah Powless," he said, and shook her hand. "How'd you get your hair that shade of blue?"

Shirley put her hands up to her short, puffy hair. "It's a rinse. Supposed to bring out the highlights in white hair. Don't you like it?" Shirley looked worried.

"Oh yeah, I like it fine. Goes with your dress," and he painted at the bright blue material. Shirley relaxed.

"I just retired from my job," Shirley said. "I was a schoolteacher. Powless. . . Powless. Is that a Mohawk name?"

"Yep. How'd you know?"

"My sister married a man from Six Nations. I guess I heard the name there. Maybe we're related!"

"Well, I never seen a Mohawk with blue hair, but then, I never seen a lot of things." Elijah shifted the sacks on his lap. "Whitefish from the Bay. You can't get this kind of fish in Detroit. I caught it myself. My twin granddaughters live there, in Detroit, but they don't fish. Too busy, I guess. And this fry bread was made by their mother." Taking a round slab out of the bag, he offered it to Shirley.

She took a bite and rolled her eyes heavenward to indicate her pleasure. "This is good bread, Elijah. My sister makes it, but not as good as this. You tell that daughter of yours that she is an excellent cook."

"She is a good cook. Guess you can tell," and he pointed to his round belly, straining against his white shirt. He had dressed very carefully for this trip. In addition to his white dress shirt, he had on the new brown corduroy pants with the cuff smartly turned up. He was wearing his turtle bolo tie and had gotten a fresh haircut just the day before. He ran his hand through his greying short hair. It felt good. He would look sharp for the twins.

He glanced at Shirley who was having a hard time keeping her eyes open. She smiled, "I guess I'll take a little nap. I was up most of the night, too excited to sleep."

"Well, you gotta be fresh for that boyfriend."

Shirley giggled and settled in her seat. She closed her eyes.

Elijah looked out the window. It was so pretty, the day. The trees were turning color, shedding their green and taking on red and gold. Elijah felt very content to be on this bus, riding to see his twins, looking out the window at the beautiful trees, the cornfields, the occasional hawk sitting on a fence post. The crows were having a good day in the fields. They swooped in a great body to scavenge among the corn.

Elijah looked around at the other passengers. He wondered where they were going, what they were going to do when they got there. "Curiosity killed the cat," his wife had always said. Elijah retorted that he wasn't a cat and *his* curiosity had kept him going this long, Edith. He missed her to this day. She was a good and pretty woman. The twins looked like her. That special look on their faces, a look of excitement, like each day was going to bring a surprise. Even when she was dying, Edith had that look on her face. Edith. Elijah fell asleep.

Elijah had a dream. He was getting off the bus and there was Annie, standing with a baby in her arms. Alice stood right alongside her holding another baby. He reached for the babies and they called out, "Great-grandfather!" He held the babies, and the twins said, "These are your great-grandchildren. Twins, like us!"

He woke up and looked at Shirley who was smiling at him.

"You must have had a pleasant dream. You were grinning and laughing like you got the present of your life."

"I did. I got twins from the twins."

As they traveled, Elijah and Shirley talked. He told her about Edith. She told him about her husband, Alan.

"He wasn't good like your Edith. He was never happy with what he had. Always looking for some ship to come in. He gambled away almost every cent we had. I eventually got smart and put my earnings where he couldn't get to it. We did not have a peaceful life together. When he died, my daughter said, 'Good riddance.' I know what she meant, but it worried me that this was how she felt about her father."

"Takes more than a name to make a father. Kids don't get choices like grownups do. Mother, father, they gotta take what they get. If someone don't act like a father, why should a child love him like a daddy? You shouldn't worry about what's over. You got any grandchildren?"

Shirley shook her head no. "But my daughter is a lovely girl. She's given me a lot of pleasure in my life. I never had to worry about her for a minute."

Elijah nodded and looked out the window again. "Look, Shirley, there's a hawk comin' in on that tree! See how he hunches up and tucks his neck in? You'd never know he was there, would you? Hawks never give up. They'll chase something down till they get it. They gotta eat. None of this goin' to the store and getting' food already there. Hawks gotta work."

"Can you picture a hawk going to the supermarket and picking out its food?" Shirley laughed.

"Well, now you mention it, I can't see it. If we worked as hard as the hawk for our food, we might think twice about throwin' so much away."

Shirley sighed, "I know what you mean, Elijah. These kids today, they don't know what it's like to go hungry. They think everything grows at the supermarket."

"Lots of kids know what it's like to go hungry. You just ain't been around them. Edie and me, we used to get the kid to help in the garden. I took 'em all huntin' and fishin'. But sometimes we went hungry too. But one thing, none of them is a waster of food."

"Look Elijah, there's the sign for Windsor!"

Shirley got up to go to the washroom. She came back smelling like lilac perfume, her lipstick newly applied, her blue hair still as a board.

Elijah made his way to the washroom and came back to his seat marveling at how small the room was. "I've never seen anything like it. While I was washing my hands I thought I was going to fall in the toilet, it was so crowded in there."

Shirley gathered her things together and sat, hands folded on top of her purse. "It's been a pleasure to meet you, Elijah. You tell those twins to take good care of you, now. I hope you enjoy your vacation."

Elijah thanked Shirley and helped her to her feet. He waved good-bye and watched her get off the bus to meet her beau.

Going through customs, Elijah wondered if Alice and Annie had changed much from six months ago when he'd last seen them. Riding through the tunnel that connected Detroit to Windsor, he smiled at his foolishness. They weren't children who changed constantly. They were women now, pretty much settled into what they would look and be like.

Elijah got up when the bus stopped. As he walked down the aisle, he caught glimpses of cement and traffic. Claiming his suitcase, he looked around for the twins. He went inside the terminal and still couldn't see them. He waited, suitcase by his feet, bags in hand, and watched all the people. There were so many kinds here. Black, brown, shades in between. White faces moved around him. They were walking to the bus, from the bus, sitting in the waiting room. Faces eating food, running after children, reading the papers. Teenage boys lined up at machines where they seemed to be playing some kind of game on a screen in front of them. Security guards and police walked through the building, keeping their eyes on the teenagers.

"Is this like TV?" Elijah asked a tall young man with dark brown skin. The young man was wearing a jacket with *Nike* streaking across the front. In fact, Nike seemed to be the young man's name, for the name was on his pants, on his shoes, and emblazoned on the cap that perched on his high hair.

"This ain't TV. It's Pacman, man."

"How does it work?"

"You puts the money in here, then you gotta get all the ghosts that pop up. Ain't you never seen this before? Man, where you been?"

Elijah dug in his pockets for coins.

"Hey man, you can't play with that kinda money. You needs American money." He looked at the old man and his disappointed face. "But here, don't worry none. See that place over there? You pays them some a your money and you gets back American. Here, I show you."

He took Elijah over to the booth that said American Exchange on its sign and showed him how to do it.

"Thank you, Nike. I should have done this before I left home. Too excited I guess. Excited about seein' my twin granddaughters. Maybe I'm gettin' old."

"Aw, don't worry about it. Hey, what you call me?"

"Nike."

The young man laughed, revealing a gap between his two front teeth. "My name ain't Nike. Anyways, it's Nik*eee*, not Nike. My name's Terrance. Terrance James." and he held out his hand for Elijah to shake. "Is somebody meetin' you? You shouldn't be wanderin' around, old man like yourself. What you got in them bags?"

"Whitefish from the Bay and some fry bread. Here, have a piece." Elijah pulled out a thick round and gave it to his new friend. "Sorry I got your name wrong. But how come you got that name on your clothes? Maybe you're wearin' somebody else's? My name's Elijah. Elijah Powless."

"No, man, these are my clothes. Nike's a brand name, like the company that makes 'em. You don't know that?" Terrance laughed. "Man, where you been?"

Elijah remarked as how he'd been in Tyedinaga and this was his first trip to Detroit and he wondered where his granddaughters were.

"That ain't right. Old man like yourself at the bus stop with nobody to meet him. That ain't right. You got a number for them girls? We could call them, tell them to get their butts over here to pick up their granddaddy. That ain't right."

Terrance pulled at his lip and looked worried while Elijah went through his pockets to find the number for the twins. "Here it is."

"There's the phone over there," Terrance pointed to the booth. "I'll wait here and play me some more games."

Elijah left his bags by Terrance, who assured him he'd keep an eye out for them. He dialed the number and let it ring ten times. He hung up the phone, wondering what to do next. Then he walked back.

"They ain't home," he said to Terrance. "I don't know what could be keepin' them, but I ain't worried. Now, show me how to play this game."

Terrance finished chewing the last piece of fry bread and showed Elijah where to put his quarters and how to play the Pacman game. "This is good bread. You got a whole bag of it? That all you got to eat?"

"No, I just brought it for the twins. You can't get this kinda food in Detroit. What kinda food *do* you get in Detroit?"

"Well, you can gets chicken or ribs or MacDonald's over there. But the best food is what my mama makes. Cornbread that'll melt in your mouth! Hey man, you Mexican or somethin'?" said Terrance, studying Elijah's face.

"I'm Mohawk. Indian."

"Yeah, we got somma them around here. They have a parade sometime. Me and my friends go. Somma them guys dance and wear these fancy costumes. Very impressive. My mama say that on me daddy's side, we gots Indian blood."

"Is that right? What kinda Indian? Is your daddy from around here?"

"My daddy ain't from around nowhere. He long dead and gone I hopes. I don't know what kinda Indian. It's all the same," Terrance nodded sagely.

"Well, it ain't all the same. But then again," Elijah said, scratching his head, "maybe it is. You gotta point there, Terrance. You're a smart young man. You go to school?"

"Hell no! I ain't been in school for four years now. I quit when I was sixteen."

"Why'd you do that, a smart boy like yourself?"

"Hey man, I'm smart 'cause I ain't goin' to school. School ain't no place for Terrance James. Shit!"

"Maybe you were in the wrong school. Seems like you shoulda done real good in school." Elijah looked around the terminal. "I wonder where those twins are."

"What we gonna do, Elijah?"

"Play another game on this Pacman machine."

Terrance laughed and loaded up the quarters. They played three more games of Pacman before they noticed another man was making signals to Terrance. "I gotta go outside for a minute, Elijah. I'll tell you what. Across the street there's a bar. I know the dude who works there. They don't let you wait around here, unless you catchin' a bus. Why don't you go over there and wait. I be back here in a minute, just gotta little business to take care of. I'll wait on the twins and you can visit with Archibald. He the dude works across the street. It be alright there. He take care a you till them twins get here." Terrance shifted from one foot to the other.

"You in a hurry, Terrance? Here, take another piece of bread. I appreciate what you're doin'. Archibald, eh? I guess I am kinda thirsty. See you later."

Terrance smiled and hurried out after the man who was impatiently waiting.

Elijah stood for a few minutes, collecting his thoughts and belongings. He walked toward the door and looked out. There, across the street, just like Terrance said, was the place where he should go. FOOD & SPIRITS, the sign said.

He crossed the street, cars braking and horns blaring. A driver shouted out, "Watch where you're going, old man!"

Elijah waved and made it safely across the street and stood at the door where the FOOD & SPIRITS sign blinked on and off. He pushed on the door and went into the dark room. Music was playing from a jukebox in the corner. Two people turned to look at him when he entered the room.

Seeing the slim, dark man behind the bar, Elijah inquired, "Are you Archibald? Terrance James sent me here. Said you was a dude who'd look after me until my twins come to get me."

"I'm Archibald. What you want? What Terrance up to sendin' you here? I'll look after you, he say? Hummmpph." Archibald scratched his head, then continued to polish the glasses he had lined up in front of him.

"What does food and spirits mean? What kinda food you got here? What kinda spirits?" Elijah sat down on a stool, carefully placing his suitcase and parcels beside him.

Archibald polished the glasses, holding one up to the dim light, then polishing some more. "Just what it say. We got sandwiches, we got burgers, we got fries, we got drinks. What'll it be old-timer? And how'd you get my name from Terrance?" Archibald stared at Elijah. "Don't seem like nobody Terrance James would know."

"I met Terrance at the bus station. A smart young man. He played on the Pacman machine, and he told me his daddy was an Indian, like me."

"Hummmpph. What'll it be, old-timer?"

"Oh, I guess I'll have one a them pops. Ginger ale. I got some fry bread here. Have a piece."

Archibald looked suspiciously at the round hunk of bread offered to him. His brown eyes stared at Elijah. He shook his head no, his large Afro glinting from the light behind the bar. His dark brown skin reminded Elijah of the color of tea, nice and strong. Archibald's skin was smooth and unlined except for a scar running up his left eyebrow to his hairline. "One Vernor's comin' up."

He poured the ginger ale into a glass filled with ice. As he set it in front of Elijah he asked, "What kinda bread is that? Where you comin' from that you met Terrance at the bus? You waitin' on somebody?"

"This is fry bread, made by my daughter-in-law. I just come down from Tyendinaga. My twin granddaughters were supposed to meet me, but something seems to have held them up. Don't worry, they'll be here." Elijah took a long swallow from his glass. "Deeeelicious!"

"Oh, I ain't worryin'," Archibald stated. "It just seem you not the kinda man that Terrance would run with. Where's this Tidaga place?"

"Tyendinaga. It's an Indian place, very pretty. It's my home." He indicated the brown bag at his side. "I got whitefish here from the Bay. We eat a lot of it. I brought it for the twins 'cause they don't get this kinda food here."

"You got that right. You from a reservation, huh? I never met no Indian from a reservation. Give you a little rye to sweeten that ginger ale?"

Elijah held up his hands. "No, my drinkin' days are over. I'm eighty years old and stick with pop these days. So Archibald, my name is Elijah. Elijah Powless. What kinda spirits you got in this place?"

"Huh. The only kinda spirits what live here is whiskey spirit, gin spirit, and rum spirit. I'm pleased to meet you, Elijah." He held out his hand. "Maybe they be other spirits, too. I ain't taken inventory lately." Archibald laughed, and the woman sitting next to Elijah giggled.

"This here's Alana. Alana here's our spirit from the bus station. She hang out here when she ain't over there."

His eyes adjusted to the lack of light in the bar, Elijah turned to smile at the woman sitting next to him. She was smiling back, her bright pink lips opened over small, white teeth. Her skin was the color of unfinished pine, Elijah thought, and her hair was the blondest and curliest he'd ever seen. Curls were draped over her shoulders and tumbling down her back. She was wearing purple eye shadow that made her brown eyes look like wet silk. Two pinks spots, the size of half dollars, were painted on her cheeks. Her black shirt was very short and kept sliding up her legs, revealing purple garters around her thighs. Elijah looked away, lest Alan think him impolite to be staring at those purple garters.

"Hey, Elijah, how you doin'?" Alana held out her fingers for Elijah to touch. "So you a real Indian, Elijah? My, my, I never met one before. Imagine, in this bar, I be sittin' next to a real Indian. My, my."

Elijah shook Alana's fingers and offered her a piece of fry bread.

"This look like fry cake, don't it Archibald? Fry cake like my grandmamma used to made." She took a bite, and her face expressed delight. "This is so good! Elijah, what you doin' carryin' sacks a fry cake around town? What's them twins thinkin' of, lettin' you wander 'round this city with a bag a fry cakes? It ain't safe!"

"It ain't their fault, Alana. I don't know what could have happened to them. But I ain't worried, yet. Do you know my twins, Alice and Annie? My granddaughters. Very pretty girls. They look like their grandmother, my Edie."

"How come Edie ain't with you, 'Lijah?" Archibald asked.

"Oh, she's been dead a long time. Cancer."

"Terrible," Alana whispered. "My mama had cancer. She had a lot of pain. I hope Edie didn't have no pain like that!"

"She did. But the place Edie's at now, I know she's happy there. No pain, just pretty things to see and all her relatives hangin' out there. Right before she died, she took my hand and said, 'Elijah, it's beautiful. It's beautiful.' Then she died. Edie was a pretty woman, so I can't imagine that the spirit place wouldn't be too."

"Ain't that beautiful," Alana sighed.

"How come Archibald said you was the spirit of the bus stop, Alana?"

"Oh him! He teasin' you," Alana giggled. "I ain't no spirit. Just a workin' girl. I work over at the bus stop sometime. I works here sometime."

"What do you do? I was a janitor when I was younger," Elijah took another sip from his glass.

Alana looked at Elijah, her silk eyes widening. "Honey, I just told you I was a workin' girl. I work the streets. Hustle. Workin' girl, workin' girl! I'm the spirit of the workin' girls!"

Archibald laughed, a rich baritone rumble coming through his throat. "Then I must be the spirit-keeper. The keeper of all the spirits in this here bar!"

Elijah looked at Archibald. "I like that. The spirit-keeper of the bar. It suits you. You look like the keeper of the spirits."

Archibald checked his reflection in the mirror behind the bar. "Well, maybe. But here, have another pop on me. Alana? Another of the same?" He busied himself with getting fresh napkins and clean glasses.

Alana checked her watch. "I guess I could stand another. It getting cold out there."

The door opened and a white man in a suit walked in. His eyes roamed around the bar and settled on the three faces looking at him. He turned around and went out the door.

Archibald laughed. "He don't like the color of the spirits in this here bar!" They laughed together, Alana's high-pitched giggle gloating above them.

"What spirit are you, Elijah? If I'm the spirit of the workin' girl, and Archibald here's the spirit-keeper, then what are you?"

Elijah thought and took another swallow of his pop. "I guess you could call me the old Indian spirit. Put me up on the shelf with the whiskey spirits. I'll be the old Indian spirit."

They laughed, Archibald slapping his hand on the counter, Alana's pink cheeks moving and bobbing, Elijah's shoulders heaving and swaying.

"But still," Alana's voice was serious, "I read a book about Indians and they could see things. They had ceremonies and holy places. And they communicated with the other world." Alana shivered and pulled her rabbit coat up around her shoulders.

"Well, what's so unusual about that?" Elijah wanted to know. "It's just knowin' what to say and what to do when you meet up with somebody that ain't from your part of town."

"You got that right, 'Lijah," Archibald was nodding his head emphatically. "It happen all the time in here. Sometime I wonder if what I seen ain't from another world! And what I sees, my own eyes don't believe it!" He wiped the counter with his cloth.

Alana laughed, "Well, that true, that true. Some a my customers from another planet." She turned her face to Elijah. "But still, Indians *is* special. You all *see* things."

"We only see what's there. Nothin' special about that. But we've been around for a long time. This is our home, has been for millions of years. Guess you could say we're familiar with all that's around us. Your people didn't get the chance to be familiar yet. You was brought here without your say-so. We just always been here. It's different in the city, though. I worry about the twins. They don't fish, they don't get to see the hawks. I bet some days, they don't even see the sky!" He shook his head and took another sip.

Alana grabbed Elijah's hand. "But listen, Elijah, we got falcons livin' right here in the city, I seen it on the TV. They brought these here peregrine falcons to live on a tall buildin'. And they live there, and they had babies, right there on the ledge of that buildin'. Imagine that! Those big, ole birds livin' in this city. It ain't so bad here, if you just look up." Alana smoothed her blonde curls, lit a cigarette, and sipped her drink. "It ain't so bad here."

"I saw one a them birds once," Archibald remarked. "Didn't know what the hell it was! Thought it be some kinda vulture, then down on me. Like to scare me to death. It flew down and grabbed a pigeon right off the street. Right in front of me. Damn! I come into work, shakin' in my shoes, and told Alana here about it. She say it musta been one a them falcons. I was damn glad to hear it. Thought it was a messenger, bringin' me a warnin' bout my sinful life!" He polished the counter, making large circles in the wood.

"Don't seem to me that the spirit-keeper would have such a sinful life. You look like a good man to me." Elijah squinted at Archibald. "Yeah, you look like a good man to me. That falcon was tellin' you so. It ain't everybody gets to see one. A shy bunch, those falcons. They don't mix with the rest of us."

"Aw, I don't know 'bout that." Archibald said, making larger circles with his cloth.

"Well, I do. And I says he is a good man," Alana spoke up. "He always got a drink waitin' on me when I too cold or too tired to work no more. He let me stay here, when I just *can't* go out anymore. When I had my little girl, Archibald watch her when I gotta go out and hit the streets. Archibald a good man . . .but my baby die."

"Aw, Alana. I didn't do nothin'. I didn't do half the things I shoulda to keep you and the baby safe."

Alana waved away his protest. "You a good man. You just don't like anybody sayin' so."

Elijah touched Alana's hand. "I lost two of my babies. Only they was grown boys and they moved away. I never saw them till they came home dead. I grieve for you, Alana."

Alana's hand shook. She moved her fingers up to her eyes, surprised at the tears dropping onto the counter. "She were only a year old. She got some kinda sickness. I took her to the doctor, but he say she be alright. Just give her some aspirin. I give it to her, but the sickness don't go away. She just get worse! She die one night, in my arms. I was rockin' her and singin' to her, and she just go, like that. It were a long time ago, but it seem like it happen just last night. I'm rockin' and singin' and she die. She die. I never had me no more kids. What for? They die too." She got up and went to the jukebox. She stood there, her face hard-edged in the colored lights.

Archibald looked at Elijah. "She don't talk much about that. Hell, what's to talk about? One years old. One years old! Them doctors oughta be shot, that's what I got to say about it." He turned his back on Elijah and started to polish the glasses.

Elijah walked over to Alana and touched her face. "When they brought my boys' bodies back home, I thought I'd go crazy with all the hurt inside me. Edie never said a word. She just kissed them, then she went outside and walked. She was gone for hours. I was afraid, thought I was goin' to lose her too. But she came back. She was walkin', she said, and found a bird nest that had fallen from a tree. She climbed the tree to put the nest up in the branches. See, there was two little chicks in that nest. Ugly little things, Edie said. No feathers, just those bare little bodies and big hungry beaks. After puttin' the nest back, Edie hid and waited for the mother. She was scared the mother wouldn't come back, or if she did, she wouldn't go near 'cause Edie had touched the nest. Well, she waited and waited, and the mother came back with a mouth full of worms and fed those babies. Then Edie walked home. She said she felt better 'cause at least somewhere, there was babies that were O.K. My Edie, she was somethin'. When I saw her walkin' toward the house, my heart felt like bustin'. Just the sight of her made me think I could handle all that hurt inside me. My baby boys. They were twins, too. Never did a thing without the other one. I guess maybe it was a good thing they died together. That's what Edie said. One couldn't live without the other. I blamed myself too. Shoulda done this, shoulda done that. Just like you, Alana. But I bet you was a good mother. I can see it."

Alana lifted her head, the lights from the jukebox making patterns on her face. "I loved her, you know? She was a little angel in my life. Like a light, you know? I wish I knew that Edie. You must miss her somethin' fierce." They walked back to the counter and sat down. Archibald still had his back to them but was watching them in the mirror.

"I miss her, yes. I miss my boys. But they're still here," he pointed to his chest. "Somewhere here. And I see Edie every once in a while. She keeps an eye on me. I hear her too. She calls, *Elijah, Elijah.* That sweet voice callin'."

"I know! My Cherry Marie, she call me too! She were learnin' to talk and she say, *Mama, Mama,* all the time. I laugh at her. "Don't you know no other words?" I say to her. *Mama, Mama.* I hear that voice, my Cherry Marie callin' me. *Mama.* I hear her and just want to follow that little voice. *Mama.*"

"Don't you be followin' no voices, you hear?" Archibald whirled around and slapped his hand on the wooden surface. "You don't be followin' no voices what call you. You gotta stay here. You alive woman, and she dead. You can't be followin' no voices." Archibald's eyes were red-rimmed and angry. "Aw, Alana, Alana." He put out his hand and touched her face. His voice became soft, "Don't follow no voices. Please, Alana."

Alana brought her hand up to Archibald's. "I won't be followin' her. I just like to hear that voice. Cherry Marie, my baby girl."

Elijah looked away from the two people. Talking about Edie, Cherry Marie, and his baby boys made him lonely, made him long for the sweet faces of the twin girls he loved so much. He felt a hand on his shoulder.

"Don't be feelin' bad, Elijah," Alana said.

"Oh, I ain't feelin' bad, just a little lonesome for my twins. But you know, it's good to talk about death. It's funny, we treat life like it ain't no big deal when it's the biggest deal there is. And we get scared to talk about death. It's just the everyday, death is. Here, have another piece of bread. When you bite into somethin' like this, you know how good life is." He handed a piece to Alana and took one for himself.

Alana took tiny bites of her bread and said, "Them twins be takin' a long time getting' here. You need a place to stay? I got a place. It clean and warm. Shame on them girls! This here town's not a safe one. Them girls shouldn't be lettin' their grandpa be wanderin' the streets. God knows what could happen!"

"It seems pretty safe to me." Elijah smiled.

Archibald chuckled, "Well, you lucky this time."

"I think I'm pretty lucky. Meetin' you two spirits, I'd say I was a lucky man."

Feeling around in his pockets for change, Elijah announced that he'd call the twins' number again. He went to the phone booth and began dialing.

The door opened and Terrance walked in, ushering Alice and Annie into the bar.

"Grandfather!" the twins shouted and ran to hug him. "There was a terrible accident on the freeway," Alice began.

"No, no, not us," Annie reassured her grandfather.

"We didn't know what to do."

"We were so worried you'd be sitting in that bus station all alone."

"I can't tell you the thoughts that were going through . . ."

"My head," Annie finished.

"You tell the story, Terrance," Alice said, holding on to her grandfather and squeezing his arm.

"Well, I finished my business and went back inside the station, just like I told you I would. I'm standin' there and in walks twins, lookin' worried. I goes up to them and says, you lookin' for Elijah?' They don't wanna say, not that I blames them! I told them you was across the street, waitin' on them. But they was nervous like. Can't blame them! But I finally told them what you looks like, that we play Pacman, and you give me a piece of bread. They looked at me like I was crazy, man! Pacman? Grandfather? they say. But it were the bread what did it. They say nobody givin' away bread but Grandfather. Must be him! So they follows me over here to Al's Bar, and here we is."

Alice and Annie laughed, and Annie poked Terrance in the ribs. "Pacman! Grandpa, when did you learn to play Pacman?"

"Today."

For some reason that made the twins laugh even harder.

"Here girls, I want you to meet my friends. Alana. Archibald. We've had a good time here."

Alice and Annie shook hands with Archibald. "Pleased to meet you ladies." Their eyebrows raised only slightly at the sight of Alana while shaking her hand.

Alana said, "So these the famous twins we been hearin' 'bout all night. They're very pretty, Elijah. You must be one proud granddaddy. Girls, your granddaddy's the nicest man. But I 'spect you know that already. I'm very pleased to meet you. Such beautiful hair," and she pointed to the twins' black, shining locks.

"Thank you," said Alice. "Uh . . . I. . ."

"Think you have lovely hair too," Annie finished.

"Oh, girls, it just a wig!" Alana touched the blonde curls and looked pleased.

Archibald lay down his polishing cloth. "What'll it be ladies? Drinks on me. Anybody know 'Lijah, they welcome here anytime."

Alice and Annie looked at each other, looked at their grandfather, looked at each other again, and laughed. "We'll have a beer."

Terrance went to the jukebox and turned on the music. Koko Taylor's pounding voice came blasting out. Terrance snapped his fingers and started singing along.

"Girls, I had a dream on the bus. You were holdin' babies in your arms. They were twins, just like you."

"Oh Grandpa, we don't have any babies. At least not yet. Annie has applied, but we don't know yet."

"Well, that's why I came here. I thought I could help in gettin' you those babies. These Natives down here, they'd listen to an old man like me, now wouldn't they? I dreamed about twin babies, and I'm here to find them for you."

The twins choked a little on their drinks but smiled at their grandfather. "We'll see, Grandpa."

"Yes, we will. Now, I brought whitefish from the Bay. Hope it's still frozen. Your mother made you this fry bread. Alana calls it fry cakes. You liked it, didn't you Alana?"

Alana nodded her agreement. "Just like my grandmamma used to make."

Elijah opened the sack. "There's plenty here. Just help yourself."

Terrance was the first one to dip into the bag. "Man, I been dreamin' 'bout this here fry bread since this afternoon. This is good bread!" He chewed ecstatically.

Even Archibald helped himself to a piece. "This *is* like fry cake. I'll be. You tell your mom she make good bread," he told the twins.

They assured him they would relay the message. They hugged their grandfather. "We're so glad you're here. Safe and sound."

"Why wouldn't I be?"

Elijah was very happy. Sharing food was the best thing people could do together. He was anxious to start on this adoption business, but for now, he was content to be with his friends and his twins, eating, laughing.

Outside the sign blinked off, then on. FOOD & SPIRITS. FOOD & SPIRITS. Inside there were music, stories, good food, and friends. Elijah was content.

Turtle Gal[1]

Sue Linn's mama was an Indian. She never knew from where, only that Dolores wore a beaded bracelet: yellow, blue, and green beads woven into signs. Burnt out from alcohol and welfare, Dolores gave up late one afternoon, spoke to her daughter in an unknown language, and put the bracelet around her girl's skinny wrist where it flopped over her hand. She turned her face to the wall and died. November 4, 1968.

Sue Linn watched her mother die, knowing by instinct that it was better this way. Better for Dolores. But her child mind, her nine-year-old mind, had not yet thought of the possibilities or penalties that lay in wait for little girls with no mother. She thought of her friend, James William Newton, who lived across the hall. She went and got him. He walked Sue Linn back to the room where her mother lay dead. "Lord, lord, lord, lord," the old man chanted as he paid his respects, covering the still-warm woman with the faded red spread. His tired eyes, weeping, looked down on the child standing so close to him. "Go get your things now, little gal. Bring everything you got. Your clothes, everything."

With his help, Sue Linn removed all traces of herself from the darkening apartment. James William made a last, quick search, then told the child to say good-bye to her mama. He waited in the hall, his face wrinkled and yellowish. His hand trembled as he reached into his pants pocket for his handkerchief, neatly folded. He shook the thin, white cloth and brought it to his eyes where he wiped the cry, then blew his nose.

Sue Linn stood beside the bed she and her mother had shared for as long as the girl could remember. She pulled the spread from her mother's face and looked intensely at Dolores. Dolores' face was quieter, younger looking. Her broad nose seemed somehow more delicate, and her dark lashes were like ink marks against her

---

1 My thanks to Tom King for the title suggestion.

smooth, reddish cheek. Sue Linn felt a choking move from her stomach up through her heart, her lungs, her throat and mouth. With an intake of harsh breath, she took a lock of her mother's black hair in her small fist. She held on, squeezing hard, as if to pull some last piece of life from her mother. She let go, turned away, and closed the door behind her. James William was waiting, his arms ready to hold her, to protect her.

Together, they opened his door, walked into the room that was welcoming and waiting for their presence. African violets sat in a row along the windowsill, their purple and blue flowers shaking from the force of the door being closed. Sue Linn went to touch the fuzzy heart leaves, wondering once again what magic the old man carried in him to grow these queer, exotic plants in the middle of a tired, dirty street.

James William put aside the bag filled with Sue Linn's belongings and told the child to sit in his chair while he went to call the ambulance. "Don't answer the door. Don't make no sounds. Sit quiet, little gal, and I be's back in a wink." He hugged the child and went out the door.

Sue Linn sat on James William's favorite chair, a gold brocade throne with arms that curved into high, wide wings. She stared out the window. She looked past the violets, past the ivy hanging in a pot attached to threads, dangling fresh and alive in front of the glass. She looked onto the street, the avenue that held similar apartment buildings, large and grey. Some had windows knocked out, some had windows made bright by plastic flowers. Some had windows decorated with a cross and Jesus Is My Rock painted on from the inside. The Salvation Army complex stood low and squat, the lights beginning to be turned on, bringing a softening sheen to the beige cement. The air was cold, the people on the street pulling their coats and jackets closer to their bodies as they walked, hunched over in struggle past the Chinese restaurants, the grocery, the bars, the apartments. Cars made noise-the noises of rust, of exhaust pipes ready to fall off, of horns applied with angry hands. Buses were unloading people, doors opening to expel faces and bodies of many shapes and colors. The avenue seemed to wander forever in a road of cement, tall buildings, people, machines, eventually stopping downtown, caught up in another tangle of streets and boulevards.

James William walked down the three flights of stairs to the payphone in the lobby. He called the operator to report the dead woman, walked back up the three flights of stairs, his thoughts jumping and beating against his brain as his heart lurched and skipped from the climb. When he entered his room the child turned to look at him. "They be here soon, child. Now we not lettin' on you here with me. We be very quiet. We lets them medical peoples take care a things. We don't say one word. Ummhmm, we don't say a word."

He came to the window and watched for the ambulance that eventually came screaming to the curb. Two white men, their faces harried and nervous, got out of the ambulance and entered the building. A police car followed. The cops went into the building where the super was arguing with the medics.

"I don't know nothin' about a dead woman! Who called you? Who did you say she was?"

The officers hurried things along, the super angrily getting out his keys. "If it's 3D, then it's that Indian. She's all the time drinkin' and carryin' on. Her and that sneaky, slant-eyed kid ain't nothing' but trouble. Who did you say called in? Nobody let on to me!"

On the third floor, cops, medics, and super formed a phalanx around the door to 3D. Knocking and getting no answer, they unlocked the door and entered the room. Up and down the hall, doors were opened in cracks. Eyes looked out, gathering information that would be hoarded and thought about, then forgotten.

"Anybody know this woman?" the cops shouted in the hall.

Doors closed. Silence answered. One of the cops pounded on a door. A very old woman opened it, a sliver of light behind her.

"Do you know this woman in 3D? When was the last time you saw her?"

Her dark brown face resettled its lines as she spoke. "I don' know her. She was an Injun lady. One a them Injuns from out west, I guess. I don' know nothin'."

The officer waved his hand in disgust. He and his partner started down the stairs, their heavy black shoes scratching the steps, the leather of their holsters squeaking as the rubbed against the guns.

James William stood, his ear pressed to the door. Sue Linn continued to stare out the window. There were sounds of feet moving away, sounds of hard breathing as the body of Dolores was carried down the three flights of stairs into the cold November twilight.

James William Newton turned from the door. He was eighty years old. He was a singer of the blues. He was the Prince of Georgia Blues. He was Sweet William. He went to the kitchenette and put the kettle on to boil. He moved slowly to the cupboard, taking out a pot and settling it on the tiny stove. Everything surrounding Sweet William was small and tiny like him. The table, covered in blue oilcloth, was just big enough for two. Little wooden chairs were drawn tight to the edge of the table, waiting for his hands to arrange the seating. The one window in the kitchenette was hung with starched white curtains trimmed in royal blue rickrack. A single wall was papered in teapots and kettles, red and blue splashed on a yellow background. The wall was faded from age but still looked cheerful and surprising. A cupboard painted white held thick dishes and the food. Rice, red beans, spices, cornmeal, salt, honey, and sugar. A cardboard box placed on the cracked yellow linoleum contained potatoes and onions, the papery skins sometimes falling to the floor, coming to rest by the broom and dustpan leaning against the teapot wall.

On the first night of Sue Linn's new life, she watched Sweet William work in the kitchen, her eyes following his round body as he walked the few steps across the linoleum, taking leaves out of a tin box, placing them in a brown pot, pouring the whistling water over the tea. He replaced the lid on the teapot, removed a tea cozy from a hook, and placed this over the pot. The child, ever fascinated by Sweet William's routine, his fussy kitchen work, his hands dusting and straightening, felt comforted by the familiar activity. Often James William made supper for the girl. Cooking up the rice, a towel wrapped around his fat waist, mashing the potatoes, adding canned milk and butter. Sometimes, there was ham hocks or chitlins. The hot, pungent dishes were magic, mage from Sweet William's hands and the air and salt.

James William sang quietly as he busied himself with the pot of soup. His eyes grabbed quick looks toward the chair and the thin, golden child who watched him with blank eyes. Little folds of flesh covered her eyelids which rapidly opened and closed. Sitting like that, so still, her eyes blinking, blinking, she reminded the old man of a turtle he'd seen a long time ago, home in Georgia.

Poking around in the marsh, he and his friends had found a spotted turtle upside-down, struggling to put itself right. He had picked up the turtle and looked at its head, pulling in, eyefolds closing over the eyes in panic, opening, closing, staring at him. He had set the turtle on its legs, where it continued on. The boys had laughed at the creature's slow journey. James William remembered the turtle, remembered his friends—the sweetness of them. Memories like this appeared in a haze. When they came to him, he clutched at them, holding onto each moment—afraid he would never see them again. He stood in the kitchenette and recalled the day of the turtle. He called forth the weather, so hot and lush, you could hold the air in your hand and feel it wet on your skin. He called forth the smell of the marsh—a green smell, a salty smell. He recalled the reeds, pulled from the mud and stuck between their lips, the taste of bitter grass mingling with another taste of sweet—like the stick of licorice his daddy had once brought him from town. He tried to call forth his friends, their · names, their brown-and-tan colors, but the memory was fading. Yet, he remembered the black skin of Isaac, his best friend of all. Remembered when Isaac held his arm, the thin fingers spread out looking like molasses spilled against his own yellow, almost white-looking arm. Isaac.

"Isaac?"

Stirring the soup, he sang bits of song culled from memories of his mama, church, and memories of the band—Big Bill and the Brown Boys. Tunes spun from his lips. Notes and chords played in his throat, starting somewhere in his mind, trickling down through his scratchy voice box, coming out round, weeping, and full. Sweet William sang, his face shifting as he wove the music in and out of his body. His head moved and dipped. His shoulders jerked and shrugged to emphasize a word, a phrase. To Sue Linn, it was as pleasurable to watch Sweet William sing as it was to listen. His words and music were almost always the same. Words that came from a heartache, a home with no furniture.

"Lord, what I gonna do with this here child? Now listen up, girl. You gonna be my little gal. We be mama and little gal. We be a family. Ummhmm, anybody ask, you be mine. It ain't gonna be easy. Old James William here, he gots to think of some heavy talkin' to fool them peoples what be snoopin' around here. Them government types. Yes ma'am. James William gots to think of some serious talk. Lord! Old man like myself with a child. A baby! I tells you, you know I never be's married. Leastwise, not no marriage like the government peoples thinks is right. Just me and Big Bill, movin' with that band. Me bein' a fool many a time over some sweet boy what talks with a lotta sugar but don' make no sense. But that Big Bill, he were some man. Always take me back, like I never did no wrong. Yes ma'am. I be a fool for a pretty boy. But I always got a little work. Workin' on them cars sometime. Child, I swear the metal in my blood! I still hear that noise. Whoo, it like to kill me! That noise, them cars hurryin' along the line, waitin' for a screw here, a jab there. But I worked it. I worked it. Yes I did. And me and Big Bill, we make a home. Yes we did. We did. And before the sugar and the high bloods get him, we make a home. We was a family that fine man and me. Ummhmm.

"Now look at her sit there with them turtle eyes. She can't talk. Now listen here, baby. You mama at rest now, bless her sorry little life. You got you another kinda mama now. I take care my baby. You mama so peaceful now. With angels and the Indians. She make that transition over, ummhmm. She be happy. Now, I gots to make this here turtle gal happy. You gots to cry sometime, child. Honey lamb, you gots to cry! If you don' grieve and wail, it get all caught up in you, start to twist your inside so bad. Girl! It hurt not to cry. You listen to this old man. Sweet William, he know what he talkin' 'bout."

I sing because I'm happy
I sing because I'm free
His eye is on the sparrow
And I know he watches me.

The old man begins his song in a whisper. As he ladled out the soup into bowls, he switched from hymn to blues, the two fitting together like verse and chorus. He nodded his head toward the child, inviting her to sing with him. Sue Linn's thin voice joined James William's fat one,

Heaven's cryin', seem like the rain keep comin' down
Heaven's cryin', seem like the rain keep comin' down
That heaven don't let up
Since my baby left this mean ole town.

They sang together. They sang for Dolores. They sang for Big Bill. They sang for each other. Blues about being poor, being colored, being out of pocket. Blues about home—that sweet, hot, green-and-brown place. Home was a place where your mama was, waiting on a porch, or cooking up the greens. Home was where you were somebody. Your name was real, and the people knew your name and called you by that name. It was when you left that home that your name became an invisible thing. You got called new names—*Nigger, Bitch, Whore, Shine, Boy.* It was when you left that home you started to choke on your name and your breath and a new kind of blues was sung.

The old man came from the kitchen and picked the child up in his arms, set her on his lap in the brocade chair, covered them with his special afghan, and the two rocked and swayed.

"She like a bird, no weight on her at all, at all. I *do* likes a rock in this old chair. It help a person think and study on things what ails us. Yes ma'am, just a rockin' and a studyin' on them things."

Sue Linn's tears began. Soon she sobbed, the wails moving across the room, coming back in an echo. James William sang, crooned, wiped her eyes and his with the dry palms of his hands.

"My baby. My turtle gal. Lord, I remember my own mama's passin'. It hurt so bad. She were a good woman, raisin' us ten kids. My daddy workin' his body to an early grave. It hurt when a mama die. Seem like they should always just go on bein' our mama. You mama, she try her best. She were a sad woman. She love you, little gal. And I loves you. We be a family now. Big Bill! You hears that? A family. Sue Linn Longboat and James William Newton. Now ain't they gonna look twice at this here family? I tell you. I tell *you!* It be alright, my baby girl. It be alright."

Sue Linn stopped crying as suddenly as she had started. Her thin face with the slanted eyes, small nose, and full lips subdued itself. "But Sweet William, I hear people talk about heaven. My mom didn't believe in it, but where will she go now? I don't know where she is. And sometimes . . . sometimes she said she wished I never was born."

The girl stared into the old man's face, trusting him to give her the answers. Trusting him to let her know why she ached so much, why she always felt alone and like a being who didn't belong on this earth. His skin was smooth, except for the cracks around his eyes and down his cheeks, ending at the corners of his mouth. His eyes were brown and yellow and matched the color of his skin, like mottled corn, covered with hundreds of freckles. He had few teeth except for a startlingly white stump here and there. When he opened his mouth to sing, it looked like stars on a black map. His lips were wide and brown. His nose was flat, the nostrils deep.

"Baby, I don' know 'bout no heaven. My mama truly believed it. But I think this here story 'bout pearly gates and all is just a trick. Seem like they ain't nothin' wrong with this here earth. The dirt gonna cover your mama and that be alright with her. She miss the sky and the wind and the land. Told me plenty a times. Seem like, compared to that heaven where the peoples hang playin' harps and talkin' sweet, this here earth ain't so bad. You mama, she be mighty unhappy in a heaven where they ain't no party or good lovin' goin' on. Seem like that heaven talk just a way to gets the peoples satisfied with the misery they has to bear in this here world. Once you gets to thinkin' that a reward waitin' on you for bein' poor and colored, why it just beat you down more. You don' stops to think 'bout doin' somethin' 'bout it right here, right now. Ummhmm, them white peoples, they thinks a everything. But there be a lot they don' know. Everything don' always mean *every thing!* I do believe Dolores more at rest in the brown dirt. And lord, child, from jump every mama wish her children never be born sometime! That's a face. Ummhmm. Honey, she love you. She just too full a pain to remember to *tell* you.

It just like me and Big Bill. Why, they be days we forgets to say, 'Big Bill, you my onliest one. James William, you sure one fine man.' Then you gets to thinkin', hey, this man don't love me no more!

and you gets afraid to ask, 'cause you thinkin' that's *his* duty to remember. Then you gets mad and sad all together and it get all mixed up and then you speakin' in shortness and evil kinda ways. You forgets that everybody be carryin' his own pain and bad things. The disrememberin' be a thing that happen though. We be foolish, us peoples. Ain' no way getting' 'round that! Seem like, if we be perfect, we be like them white peoples up there in heaven they thinks so special. Yes, yes, we be in that white heaven, with the white pearly gates, and the white robes, and the white slippers. Child! You ever think 'bout heaven always bein' so white? Lord child! Whooo!"

He laughed and laughed, hugging Sue Linn tight, his chest rumbling in her ear. She laughed too, even though she wasn't sure she knew the joke. But it made her feel better to be sitting in Sweet William's lap, her head pressed to his heart, the afghan of bright colors covering her coldness and fright. She used to laugh with Dolores. Mostly over Dolores' mimicry of the people on the street or in the bars. She had almost become those people, so good was she at capturing a gesture, a voice, a way of holding her body. There was no meanness in the foolery, just fun, just a laugh, a present for Sue Linn.

"Now, my turtle gal, this old colored man be talkin' more than his due. I says, after a song and a good cry, they ain't nothin' better than hot soup and peppermint tea. I thinks I even gots a little banana cake saved for you."

They unfolded from the brocade chair and went to the table. The tiny, round Black man of light skin. The tiny, thin girl of gold skin and Indian hair, her body wrapped in the afghan crocheted by Sweet William's hands. As James William poured the tea, his white shirt dazzled the girl's eyes. She watched his short legs walk slowly to the stove, his small feet wearing the felt slippers he never seemed to take off. He was wearing his favorite pants—grey flannel with handsome pleats and small cuffs at the bottom. He was wearing the only belt Sue Linn had ever seen him wear—a wide alligator strip with a buckle of solid silver, round and etched with the words *Florida Everglades*. It had been a gift from Big Bill so many years ago, the date and reason for the gift were lost in James William's memory. He only remembered Big Bill's face as he handed the belt to Sweet William, the pale mocha of his skin flushing and reddening as he pushed the tissue-wrapped gift toward James William, saying, "Here, honey. For you. A gift." James William's starched, white shirt had cuffs that were turned back and fastened with silver-colored links, a red stone gleaming in the center of each piece of metal. Sue Linn stared at the stones that seemed to signal on-off-stop. Red means stop . . . .

She had learned that in school when she started kindergarten. That was four years ago. She was in third grade now, a big girl. She liked school. At least, she liked it when she went, when her mom remembered to send her. When Sue Linn felt safe to ask Dolores to braid her long hair without making the woman cry. When Dolores was in a good mood from having extra money and bought Sue Linn plaid dresses, white socks, and shoes that were shiny and had buckles instead of laces. She talked loud at these times, talked about how her baby was just as good as anybody, and anyway, she was the prettiest kid in school by far. Sue Linn had a hard time understanding this talk. Everyone in school wore old clothes and shoes with laces. It didn't make sense. Maybe it had to do with the picture magazines that showed up around the apartment. The people on the shiny pages were white and stood in funny poses. They wore fancy clothes and coats made from animals. They looked like they were playing statues, which Sue Linn had played once with the kids at school. It was a scary feeling to stop and stand so still until the boss kid said you could move. She liked it though. It made her feel like she was invisible. If she were really a statue, she'd be made out of wood or stone-something hard.

Sort of like the statues at the place her teacher, Miss Terrell, had taken them. Miss Terrell called the giant building a museum and said the statues were sculptures. She pointed out one made by a Black man. She took them to see a display case that had Indian jewelry resting on pieces of wood, only Miss Terrell called it Native American art. Sue Linn thought of her mother's beaded bracelet and stared at the glass case. It made her want to cry for a reason she couldn't even begin to think about. She remembered the Indian case for a long time after. She told her mom about it, and Dolores said it would be nice to go there; she had gone there once, she though. But they never talked about it again. No, Sue Linn was not a statue. She was bony and covered with soft, gold skin and black hair that was coarse and reached below her shoulder blades. She practiced statues at home, standing on the worn green couch, trying to see herself in the wavy mirror on the opposite wall.

"Getting stuck on yourself, honey? That's how I started. A grain of salt, honey. That's what we need to take ourselves with. We're just bones and skin, honey. Bones and skin."

The child thought her mother much more than bones, skin, and salt. She thought Dolores was beautiful and was proud to walk with her on the avenue. The day they got the food stamps was one of the best days, for a while, Dolores was sober on those days. She would sit at the card table making lists and menus. Dolores labored hard on those days, looking through her magazines, cutting out recipes for "tasty, nutritional meals within your budget. Sue Linn stayed close to her mother on days like that, fascinated by Dolores' activity.

"How would you like chicken vegetable casserole on Monday? Then on Tuesday we could have Hawaiian chicken. I found a recipe for peanut butter cookies. It says here that peanut butter is a good source of protein. Would you like Dolores to make you cookies, baby? Maybe we could make them together." Sue Linn shook her head yes and stood even closer to her mother. Shiny paper with bright colors of food lay emblazoned on the table. Sue Linn was caught by Dolores' words, her magic talk of casseroles and cookies. Writing down words that came back as food. Food was something real yet mysterious. Food was something there never was enough of. Sue Linn ate a free lunch at school. Always hungry, eating too fast, not remembering what she ate, just eating then being hungry again.

Each morning Miss Terrell asked if anyone had forgotten to eat breakfast, because she just happened to bring orange juice and graham crackers from home. Miss Terrell must be magic because there was always enough for everyone. Miss Terrell was black, almost pure black like the stone set in the school door proclaiming when it was built (1910) and whose name it was built to honor (Jeremy Comstock). Marble, yes, that's what Miss Terrell called it. Black marble, that was Miss Terrell's skin. Her hair was cut close to her head and curled tightly against her scalp. James William's hair was like this, but more bushy, and his hair was white while Miss Terrell's was black with a red cast in the sunlight. She wore red lipstick, sometimes purple to go with the dress with white and pink dots on the sash. Her clothes were beautiful. Blue skirt and red jacket. Green dress with gold buttons. Her shoes were red or black shiny stuff with pointy, pointy toes and little wooden heels. Miss Terrell was tall and big. Some of the boys whispered and laughed about Miss Terrell's "boobs." Sue Linn saw nothing to laugh about, only knowing that boys giggled about sex things. She thought Miss Terrell's chest was wonderful. It stuck out far and looked proud in a way. When she told this to Sweet William, he said, "Child, that Alveeta Terrell be a regular proud woman. Why wouldn't her chest be as proud as the rest of her? You lucky as can be to have proud Miss Alveeta Terrell be your teacher!"

One time, and it was the best time, Miss Terrell had come to school in a yellow dress over which she wore a length of material made from multicolored threads of green, red, purple, yellow, and black. She called it Kente cloth and told the class it was woven in Africa and the people, even the men, wore it every day. She said she was wearing this special cloth because it was a special day. It was a day that Black people celebrated being African, and even though they might live in all kinds of places, they had come from Africa at one time. Then she showed them a map of Africa and traced lines running from that continent to North America, to the West Indies, to South America, to just about everywhere. Amos asked, if Africa was so special, why did the people leave? Miss Terrell said that the people didn't leave because they wanted to, but because these other people—Spanish, British, American, and French—had wanted slaves to work on their lands and make things grow for them so they could get rich. And these same people killed Indians in North America to get land. And these people had captured Africans as if they were herds of animals. They had put them in chains and shipped them to lands where their labor was needed. Some Africans had died trying to escape, some from hunger, thirst, and disease, but some had stayed alive to reach the new land that was a stranger to them.

The children pondered on these facts before raising their hands to ask questions. Miss Terrell answered in her sure voice. She knew everything. She told them about Denmark Vesey, Nat Turner, John Brown, Chrispus Attucks, whose name meant *deer* because his mama had been a Choctaw Indian. She told them about Touissant L'Overture, about the Maroons in Jamaica, about Harper's Ferry. She told them about the Seminoles and Africans in Florida creating an army to fight U.S. soldiers and how they had won the fight! Sue Linn's mind was so filled with these wondrous facts, she dreamed about them that night. And it came to her in the dream that Miss Terrell was a food-giver. Her thoughts and facts were like the graham crackers she laid out on her desk each morning. They were free to take, to eat right at that moment, or to save for when one got really hungry. The next morning, Sue Linn copied down her dreams in the little notebook she carried with her everywhere. "Miss Terrell is a food-giver." She told Sweet William, who agreed.

Food stamp day. Dolores was making something out of nothing. What did it mean? Everything meant something. This she had learned on her own, from the streets, from being a kid. She wanted to talk with Dolores about this, but was too shy.

Dolores was ready. Sue Linn puttered at the table, stalling for time, prolonging the intimacy with her mother. Sue Linn was not ready for the store. *It* happened every time. Dolores got sad. The store defeated her. It was a battle to see how far down the aisles she could get before giving up. The limp vegetables, the greenish-brown meat, the lack of anything resembling the food in the magazines. Sue Linn sensed it before it happened. The faint shrug of Dolores' shoulders, the shake of her head as if clearing it from a dream. Then they proceeded fast, Dolores grabbing at things that were cheap and filling, if only for a few hours. The little girl tried calling her mother's attention to funny people in the store, or some fancy-packaged box of air and starch. Anything, *please, please,* to get that look off her mother's face. That look of fury and contempt. That look of sadness and loss. They would end up with a few things like bread, canned corn, and maybe, hamburger. All her food stamps gone, they'd put the groceries away and Dolores would go out and not return until the next day with a few dollars and a raging headache.

Dolores picked up her lists and stamps, placed them in her purse, a beige plastic bag with her initials stamped in gold letters:

D. L., Dolores Longboat. She went to the wavy mirror and, with her little finger, applied blue eye shadow because "you never know who we'll meet." She brushed her black hair until it crackled with sparks and life across her wide back. Dressed in too-tight jeans, a pink sweater frayed and unraveling at the bottom, her gold-tone earrings swinging and dancing, she defied anyone or anything to say she didn't exist. "Let's go."

Sue Linn took hold of her mother's hand and stared up at Dolores, as if to burn the image of her mama into her brain, as if to keep the scent of lily-of-the-valley cologne in her nose. The brown eyes shaded in blue looked down at her child. Dark eye watched dark eye—two females locked in an embrace of color, blood, and bewildering love. Dolores broke the intensity of the moment, cast her eyes around the apartment, committing to memory what she had to come home to. Tightening her hold on Sue Linn's hand, she said once again, "Let's go." She set the lock and the two went out into the street.

Sue Linn's eyes closed with this last memory. Her head nodded above the soup. James William rose from the table and pulled the bed down from the wall. Straightening the covers and fluffing the pillow, he made the bed ready for the child's tired body and heart. He picked her up and carried her the few feet to the bed. Taking off her shoes, he gently placed the girl under the blanket and tucked the pillow under her head. He placed the afghan at the foot of the bed, folded and neat.

James William Newton—Sweet William—went to his chair and sat in the nighttime light. He could see a piece of the moon through a crack between two buildings across the street.

"Ole moon, what you think? I gots this here child now. Them government peoples be wantin' to know where this child be. Or is they? Seem like the whereabouts of a little gal ain' gonna concern to many a them. Now, I ain't worryin' 'bout raisin' this here turtle gal. It one a them things I be prepared to do. But Moon, we gots to have a plan. I an old man. This here baby need me. Yes, ma'am. There gots to be some providin' to do. Big Bill? Is you laughin' at me? It be a fix we in. Ummhmm, a regular fix. Big Bill? I needs a little a that talk you always so ready with. Honey, it ever be a wonder to me how a man could talk so much and *still* make sense like you done! I sittin' here waitin' on you, honey. Sweet William, he waitin' on you."

He sat through the night, refilling his cup many times. His memories came and went like the peppermint tea he drank. His lips moved in conversation and song. Sometime before dawn he laughed and murmured, "Thank you, honey. You always was the bestest man." He drank his last cup, rinsed it, and set it upside-down in the sink. He settled his body on the blue davenport, the afghan pulled up to his shoulders. He looked one more time at the sleeping child, her dark hair hiding her face in sleep.

"Child, sleep on and dream. Sweet William, he here. Me and Big Bill take care of our baby, turtle gal. You be alright. Yes, ma'am, you be alright."

He closed his eyes and slept.

The Good Red Road

Journeys of Homecoming in Native Women's Writing

There are those who think they pay me a compliment in saying that I am just like a white woman. My aim, my joy, my pride is to sing the glories of my own people. Ours is the race that taught the world that avarice veiled by any name is crime. Ours are the people of the blue air and the green woods, and ours is the faith that taught men and women to live without greed and die without fear.[1]

These are the words of Emily Pauline Johnson, Mohawk writer and actor. Born of an English mother and Mohawk father, Pauline Johnson began a movement that has proved unstoppable in its momentum—the movement of First Nations women to write down our stories of history, of revolution, of sorrow, of love.

The Song My Paddle Sings

August is laughing across the sky
Laughing while paddling, canoe and I
Drift, drift
Where the hills uplift
On either side of the current swift.[2]

This is the familiar poem of Pauline Johnson, the one that schoolchildren, white schoolchildren were taught. Her love of land made her the poet she was. Yet, in reading Johnson, a non-Native might come away with the impression that she only wrote idyllic

---

1   E. Pauline Johnson as quoted in Betty Keller, *Pauline: A Biography of Pauline Johnson* (Vancouver: Douglas & McIntyre, 1981): 5.

2   E. Pauline Johnson, "The Song My Paddle Sings" in *Flint & Feather*. (Toronto: Hodder & Stoughton, 1931).

sonnets to the glory of nature, the "noble savage," or "vanishing redman" themes that were popular at the turn of the century. It is time to take another look at Pauline Johnson.

The Cattle Thief

How long have you paid us for our game? how paid us for our land?
By a *book,* to save our souls from the sins *you* brought in your other hand.
Go back with your new religion, we never have understood
Your robbing an Indian's *body,* and mocking his *soul* with food.
Go back with your new religion, and find—if find you can—
The *honest* man you have ever made from out of a *starving* man.
You say your cattle are not ours, your meat is not our meat;
When *you* pay for the land you live in, *we'll* pay for the meat we eat.[3]

It is also time to recognize Johnson for the revolutionary she was. Publicized as the "Mohawk Princess" on her many tours as a recitalist, she despised the misconceptions non-Natives had about her people. Her anger and the courage to express that anger also made her the poet she was. She was determined to destroy stereotypes that categorized and diminished her people. Breaking out of the Victorian strictures of her day, she drew a map for all women to follow. She had political integrity and spiritual honesty, the true hallmarks of a revolutionary.

The key to understanding Native women's poetry and prose is that we love, unashamedly, our own. Pauline Johnson wrote down that love. Her short stories are filled with Native women who have dignity, pride, anger, strength, and spiritual empowerment.[4]

Pauline Johnson was a Nationalist. Canada may attempt to claim her as theirs, but Johnson belonged to only one Nation, the

---

3 E. Pauline Johnson, "The Cattle Thief" in *Flint & Feather.*

4 E. Pauline, *The Moccasin Maker* (Tucson: University of Arizona, 1987).

Mohawk Nation. She wrote at great length in her poems, stories and articles about this kind of Nationalism. She had a great love for Canada, the Canada of oceans, mountains, pine trees, lakes, animals and birds, not the Canada of politicians and racism that attempted to regulate her people's lives.

In 1892, she was writing articles on cultural appropriation, especially critiquing the portrayal of Native women in the fiction of the day. She tore apart popular white writers such as Charles Mair and Helen Hunt Jackson for their depictions of Native women as subservient, foolish-in-love, suicidal "squaws." Her anger is tempered with humour as she castigates these authors for their unimaginative use of language and for their insistence on naming the Native heroines "Winona" or a derivative thereof.[5]

Pauline Johnson is a spiritual grandmother to those of us who are women writers of the First Nations. She has been ignored and dismissed by present-day critics and feminists, but this is just another chapter in the long novel of dismissal of Native women's writing.

Pauline Johnson's physical body died in 1915, but her spirit still communicates to us who are Native women writers. She walked the writing path clearing the brush for us to follow. And the road gets wider and clearer each time a Native woman picks up her pen and puts her mark on paper.

I look on Native women's writing as a gift, a give-away of the truest meaning. Our spirit, our sweat, our tears, our laughter, our love, our anger, our bodies are distilled into words that we bead together to make power. Not power *over* anything. Power. Power that speaks to hearts as well as to minds.

Land. Spirit. History, present, future. These are expressed in sensual language. We labour with the English language, so unlike our own. The result of that labour has produced a new kind of writing. I sometimes think that one of the reasons our work is not reviewed or incorporated into literature courses, (besides the obvious racism) is that we go against what has been considered "literature." Our work is considered "too political" and we do not stay in our place—the place that white North America deems

---

5 E. Pauline Johnson, "A Strong Race Opinion on the Indian Girl in Modern Fiction," originally published in the *Toronto Sunday Globe*, 22 May 1982.

acceptable. It is no coincidence that most Native women's work that gets published is done so by the small presses: feminist, leftist or alternative. These presses are moving outside the mainstream and dominant prescriptions of what constitutes good writing. The key word here is "moving." There is a movement going on that is challenging formerly-held beliefs of writing and *who* does that writing. And it is no coincidence that when our work is taught, it is being done so by Women's Studies instructors and/or those teachers who are movers and hold beliefs that challenge those of the dominant culture. This is not to say that *all* women's studies are as forward thinking as we would like. At Women's Studies conferences, the topics of discussion usually center on white, European precepts of theory and literature. I am tired of hearing Virginia Woolf and Emily Dickinson held up as the matriarchs of feminist and/or women's literature. Woolf was a racist, Dickinson was a woman of privilege who never left her house, nor had to deal with issues beyond which white dress to wear on a given day. Race and class have yet to be addressed, or if they are discussed, it is on *their* terms, not *ours*.

We are told by the mainstream presses that our work doesn't sell. To quote Chief Sealth—"Who can sell the sky or the wind? Who can sell the land or the Creator?" The few women of colour who have broken through this racist system are held up as *the* spokespeople for our races. It is implied that these women are the only ones *good* enough to "make it." These women are marketed as exotic oddities. (After all, we all know that women of colour can't write or read, eh?)

Pauline Johnson faced this racism constantly. The "Mohawk Princess" was considered an anomaly, and I can't say that things have changed all that much. I think of Pauline a lot, especially when I rise to read my stories. For like her, "My aim, my joy, my pride is to sing the glories of my own people."

Because of our long history of oral tradition, and our short history of literacy (in the European time frame) the amount of books and written material by Native people is relatively small. Yet, to us, these are precious treasures carefully nurtured by our communities. And the number of Native women who are writing and publishing is growing. Like all growing things, there is a need and desire to ensure the flowering of this growth. You see, these fruits feed our communities. These flowers give us survival tools. I would say that Native women's writing is the Good Medicine that can heal us as a human people. When we hold up the mirror to our lives, we are also reflecting what has been done to us by the culture that lives outside that mirror. It is possible for all of us to learn the way to healing and self-love.

It is so obvious to me that Native women's writing is a generous sharing of our history and our dreams for the future. That generosity is a collective experience. And perhaps this is the major difference between Aboriginal writing and that of European-based "literature." We do not write as individuals communing with a muse. We write as members of an ancient, cultural consciousness. Our "muse" is *us*. Our "muse" is our ancestors. Our "muse" is our children, our grandchildren, our partners, our lovers. Our "muse" is Earth and the stories She holds in the rocks, the trees, the birds, the fish, the animals, the waters. Our words come from the very place of all life, the spirits who swirl around us, teaching us, cajoling us, chastising us, loving us.

The first known novel written by a Native woman was *Cogewea —The Half-Blood.*[6] Written by Hum-Ishu-Ma, Okanagan Nation, in 1927, this novel depicts the difficulties of being called half-breed. Hum-Ishu-Ma concentrates on the relationship the female protagonist has with her Indian grandmother, and how Cogewea does not turn her back on her people, although she is courted and temporarily seduced by the white world. Hum-Ishu-Ma worked as a migrant labourer, carrying her typewriter everywhere with her, snatching moments to write. Again, I am reminded of Pauline Johnson and her Indian women who remain steadfast in their Aboriginal beliefs and spiritual connections to their land and people and the desire to make this truth known.

Fifty years later, Maria Campbell wrote her groundbreaking *Half-Breed,*[7] taking up the theme of despair that comes as a result

---

6   Hum-Ishu-Ma (Mourning Dove), *Cogewea, The Half-Blood* (Lincoln: University of Nebraska, 1981).

Hum-Ishu-Ma's mentor was a white man. My reading of *Cogewea* is that much of it was influenced by his perceptions, not Hum-Ishu-Ma's.

7   Maria Campbell, *Half-Breed* (Toronto: McClelland & Stewart, 1973).

of the imbalance that racism and poverty create in a people. Maria has a grandmother whose words and strength give her nurturance and hope and a way back to the Good Red Road. The Good Red Road is a way of life among Native peoples that is one of balance and continuity. Again, this seems to be the overwhelming message that Native women bring to writing. Creating a balance in their protagonists' worlds, remembering what the Elders taught, recovering from the effects of colonialism. This is not to say that Native women's writing contains "happy" endings or resolutions. In fact, to wrap things up in a tidy package is not following the Good Red Road—it's a falsehood. Perhaps this is what irritates white critics—our work is said to have no plots! If we won't conform, how can these conformist reviewers write reviews?! Perhaps the questions should be: why are critics so unimaginative in *their* writing? Why are they so ignorant of what is being written by my sisters? Why is a white-European standard still being held up as the criteria for all writing? Why is racism still so rampant in the arts?

Leslie Marmon Silko published her novel, *Ceremony,*[8] in 1976. In 1992, *Almanac of the Dead,*[9] by the same author, was published. Between those years and after, Paula Gunn Allen, Louise Erdrich, Jeannette Armstrong, Anna Lee Walters, Ella Deloria, Beatrice Culleton, Ruby Slipperjack, Cyndy Baskin, Betty Bell, Lee Maracle, Velma Wallis and Linda Hogan also published novels.[10]

---

8 Leslie Marmon Silko, *Ceremony* (New York: Viking Press, 1977).

9 Leslie Marmon Silko, *Almanac of the Dead* (New York, Toronto: Simon & Schuster, 1991).

10 Paula Gunn Allen, *The Woman Who Owned the Shadows* (San Francisco: Spinsters/ Aunt Lute, 1983); Louise Erdrich, *Love Medicine* (Toronto, New York: Bantam, 1989); Jeanette Armstrong, *Slash* (Penticton: Theytus, 1986); Anna Lee Walters, *Ghost-Singer* (Flagstaff: Northland, 1988); Beatrice Culleton, *In Search of April Raintree* (Winnipeg: Pemmican, 1983); Ella Deloria, *Water Lily* (Lincoln: University of Nebraska, 1988); Ruby Slipperjack, *Honour the Sun* (Winnipeg: Pemmican, 1987); Ruby Slipperjack, *Silent Words* (Saskatoon: Fifth House, 1992); Cyndy Baskin, *The Invitation* (Toronto: Sister Vision, 1993); Linda Hogan, *Mean Spirit* (New York: Atheneum, 1990); Lee Maracle, *Ravensong* (Vancouver: Press Gang, 1993); Velma Wallis, *Two Old Women* (New York: Harper Perennial, 1993); Betty Louise Bell, *Faces In the Moon* (Norman: University of Oklahoma Press, 1994).

In the field of autobiographical works, the number of Native women's books is outstanding. Minnie Freeman, Maria Campbell, Ruby Slipperjack, Alice French, Ignatia Broker, Lee Maracle, Madeline Katt, Florence Davidson, Mary John, Gertrude Bonnin, Verna Johnson and others[11] tell their stories for all to hear, and we become witness of the truth of Native lives. Throughout these writings, strong female images and personas are evident. The Cheyenne saying, "A Nation is not conquered until its women's hearts are on the ground," becomes a prophecy about Native women's writing. First Nations women's hearts are not on the ground. We soar with the birds and our writing soars with us because it contains the essence of our hearts.

Deep connections with our female Elders and ancestors is another truth that we witness. Grandmothers, aunties, all abound in our writing. This respect for a female wisdom is manifested in our lives; therefore, in our writing.

Poetry seems to be the choice of telling for many Native women. In our capable hands, poetry is torn from the elitist enclave of intellectuals and white, male posturing, and returned to the lyrical singing of the drum, the turtle rattle, the continuation of the Good Red Road and the balance of Earth. We write poems of pain and power, of ancient beliefs, of sexual love, of broken treaties, of despoiled beauty. We write with our human souls and voices. We write songs that honour those who came before us and those in our present lives, and those who will carry on the work of our Nations. We write songs that honour the every-day, we write songs to food; we even incorporate recipes into our work. Chrystos, Mary TallMountain,

---

11 Minnie Freeman, *Life Among the Qallunaat* (Edmonton: Hurtig, 1978); Ignatia Broker, *Night Flying Woman: An Ojibway Narrative* (St. Paul: Minnesota Historical Society, 1983); Lee Maracle, *Bobbie Lee: Indian Rebel* (1976; reprint, Toronto: Women's Press, 1990); Verna Patronella Johnston, *I Am Nokomis, Too* (Don Mills: General Publishing Ltd., 1977); Madeline Katt Theriault, *Moose to Moccasins* (Toronto: Natural Heritage/Natural History Inc., 1992); Janet Campbell Hale, *Bloodlines* (New York: Harper Perennial, 1993)l Wilma Mankiller, *Mankiller: A Chief and Her People* (New York: St. Martin's Press, 1993); Bonita Wa Wa Calachaw Nunez, *Spirit Woman* (New York: Harper & Row, 1980); Helen Pease Wolf, *Reaching Both Ways* (Laramie: Jelm Mountain Publications, 1989); Zitkala-Sa, *American Indian Stories* (Washington: Hayworth, 1921); Ida Patterson, *Montana Memories* (Pablo: Salish Kootenai Community College, 1981); Alice French, *My Name is Masah* (Winnipeg: Pequis, 1976); and *Restless Nomad* (Winnipeg: Pemmican, 1991).

Nora Danhauer, Mary Moran,[12] are just a few who have written about the joys of fry bread, salmon, corn soup and whale blubber, then turn around and give instruction for preparing these treats! To me, this is so ineffably Indian. Mouths salivating with the descriptions of our basic foods, readers are then generously offered the gift of how to do this ourselves. No wonder the critics have so much trouble with us! How could food possibly be art? How can art remain for the elite if these Native women are going to be writing recipes in poems? What will the world come to, when food is glorified in the same way as Titian glorified red hair?

There are numerous books of poetry written by Native women.[13] Our poems are being published in forward-thinking journals and magazines, although there are still the literary journals that wish to ghettoize our work into "special" issues, which, if you will notice, happen about every ten years or so. And their editors are usually white and educated in the mainstream constructs of European sensibility.

When I was asked in 1983 to edit a Native women's issue of the feminist journal, *Sinister Wisdom,* I did not expect the earthquake that *A Gathering of Spirit* would cause. Eventually, this work became a book, published in 1984, then re-issued by Firebrand Books and by Women's Press in 1989.[14] Perhaps there is a lesson here. When Natives have the opportunities to do our own editing and writing, a remarkable thing can happen. This thing is called *telling the truth for ourselves*—a novel idea to be sure and one that is essential to the nurturance of new voices in our communities. I conduct writing workshops with Native women throughout North America, and the overriding desire present in these workshops is to heal. Not just

---

12   Chrystos, "I Am Not Your Princess," *Not Vanishing* (Vancouver: Press Gang, 1988); Mary TallMountain, "Good Grease," in *The Light On the Tent: A Bridging* (Los Angeles: University of California, 1990); Nora Marks Dauenhaur, "How to Make a Good Baked Salmon," *The Droning Shaman* (Haines: Black Currant, 1985); Mary Moran, *Métisse Patchwork*, unpublished manuscript.

13   Poets include Beth Cuthand, Joy Harjo, Marie Baker (Annharte), Janice Gould, Wendy Rose, Diane Glancy, Awiakta, Elizabeth Woody, Joanne Arnott, Carol Lee Sanchez, Paula Gunn Allen.

14   Beth Brant, ed, *A Gathering of Spirit* (Sinister Wisdom Books, 1984; Ithaca: Firebrand, 1988; Toronto: Women's Press, 1989).

the individual, but the broken circles occurring in our Nations. So, writing does become the Good Medicine that is necessary to our continuation into wholeness. And when we are whole our voices sail into the lake of *all* human experience. The ripple-effect is inevitable, vast and transcendent.

There are women who are writing bilingually. Salli Benedict, Lenore Keeshig-Tobias, Rita Joe, Beatrice Medicine, Anna Lee Walters, Luci Tapahonso, Mary TallMountain, Nia Francisco, Ofelia Zepeda, Donna Goodleaf[15] are just some of the Native women who are choosing to use their own Nation's languages when English won't suffice or convey the integrity of the meaning. I find this an exciting movement within our movement. And an exciting consequence would be the development of *our own* critics, and publishing houses that do bilingual work. Our languages are rich, full of metaphor, nuance, and life. Our languages are not dead or conquered—like women's hearts, they are soaring and spreading the culture to our youth and our unborn.

Pauline Johnson must be smiling. She was fluent in Mohawk, but unable to publish those poems that contained her language. There is a story that on one of her tours, she attempted to do a reading in Mohawk. She was booed off the stage. Keeping her dignity, she reminded members of the audience that she had to learn *their* language, wouldn't it be polite to hear hers? Needless to say, impoliteness won the day.

From Pauline Johnson to Margaret Sam-Cromarty,[16] Native women write about the land, the land, the land. This land that brought us into existence, this land that houses the bones of our ancestors, this land that was stolen, this land that withers without our love and care. This land that calls us in our dreams and visions, this land that bleeds and cries, this land that runs through our bodies.

---

15 Lenore Keeshig-Tobias, *Bird Talk* (Toronto: Sister Vision, 1992); Rita Joe, *Poems of Rita Joe* (Halifax: Abenaki, 1978); Beatrice (Bea) Medicine, "Ina," *A Gathering of Spirit*; Anna Lee Walters, *Talking Indian: Reflections on Survival and Writing* (Ithaca: Firebrand, 1992); Nia Francisco, *Blue Horses For Navajo Women* (Greenfield Center: Greenfield Review, 1988); Ofelia Zepeda, unpublished manuscript; Donna Goodleaf, unpublished manuscript.

16 Margaret Sam-Cromarty, *James Bay Memoirs* (Lakefield: Waapoone Publishing, 1992).

From Pauline Johnson to Marie Baker, Native women write with humour. Even in our grief, we find laughter. Laughter at our human failings, laughter with our Tricksters, laughter at the stereotypes presented about us. In her play, *Princess Pocahontas and the Blue Spots*,[17] Monique Mojica, Kuna/Rappahannock, lays bare the lies perpetrated against Native women. And she does it with laughter *and* anger—a potent combination in the hands of a Native woman. Marie Baker, Anishanabe, has written a play that takes place on the set of an Indian soap opera, "As the Bannock Burns." Baker's characters are few—the Native star of the soap, and the new co-star, a Native woman who gives shaman lessons to wannabes. In the course of the one-act play, the star shows the would-be shaman the error of her ways under the watchful eyes and chorus of a group of women of colour. Not only does Baker poke fun at the Greek chorus concept in theatre, she turns this European device to her own and *our* own amusement in a caustic but loving way, to bring the would-be shaman to a solid understanding of herself and her own tradition.

Sarah Winnemucca, Suzette La Flesch,[18] and Pauline Johnson also left them laughing as they took their work on the road. To tell a good story, one has to be a good actor. I remember my grandad telling me stories when I was little, punctuating the sentences with movement and grand gestures, changing his facial expressions and voice. I think we are likely to witness more Native women writing for the theatre. Margo Kane has ventured into that place with her play *Moon Lodge.* Vera Manuel has written *The Spirit in the Circle,* addressing the painful past of residential schools and the painful present of alcoholism and family dysfunction. But she also posits a vision for the future out of these violent truths. Spider Woman's Theatre has been writing, producing and acting in their plays for a number of years. And Muriel Miguel, one of the Spiders, has done a one-woman show incorporating lesbian humour, Native tricksters and female history. Native women are writing the scripts for their

---

17 Monique Mojica, *Princess Pocahontas and the Blue Spots* (Toronto: Women's Press, 1991).

18 Sarah Winnemucca and Suzette La Flesch (Bright Eyes) travelled and performed in the United States, talking about their people in poetry and story, within the same timeframe as Pauline Johnson's career.

videos and directing and producing these films. How Pauline Johnson would have loved video!

As Native women writers, we have formed our own circles of support. At least once a week, I receive poems and stories in the mail, sent to me by First Nations writers I know and some I have never met. It thrills me to read the words brought forth by my sisters. This is another form our writing takes—being responsible and supportive to our sisters who are struggling to begin the journey of writing truth. The Wordcraft Circle, a mentoring program that matches up more experienced writers with our younger brothers and sisters, was born out of a Native writers' gathering held in 1992 in Oklahoma. I am currently working with a young, Native lesbian, and it moves my heart that it is now possible for lesbian Natives to give voice to *all* of who we are. Keeping ourselves secret, separating parts of ourselves in order to get heard and/or published has been detrimental to our communities and to our younger sisters and brothers who long for gay and lesbian role models. I am proud of the burgeoning Native lesbian writing that is expanding the idea of what constitutes Native women's writing.

There are my sisters who have internalized the homophobia so rampant in the dominant culture and that has found its way into our own territories and homes. These sisters are afraid and I understand that fear. Yet, I ask for a greater courage to overcome the fear. The courage to be who we are for the sake of our young and to honour those who have come before us. Courage of the kind that Connie Fife, Chrystos, Barbara Cameron, Sharon Day, Susan Beaver, Nicole Tanguay, Two Feathers, Donna Goodleaf, Janice Gould, Vickie Sears, Donna Marchand, Mary Moran, Elaine Hall, Lena ManyArrows, Shirley Brozzo and many others have displayed.[19] Writing with our *whole* selves is an act that can re-vision our world.

---

19 Makeda Silvera, ed., *Piece of My Heart* (Toronto: Sister Vision, 1991); Will Roscoe, ed., *Living the Spirit: A Gay American Anthology* (New York: St. Martin's, 1988); Connie Fife, ed., *The Colour of Resistance* (Toronto: Sister Vision, 1993); Gloria Anzaldua, ed., *This Bridge Called My Back* (Albany: Kitchen Table Press, 1981) are just four of the collections containing Native lesbian work. See also Connie Fife, *Beneath the Naked Sun* (Toronto: Sister Vision, 1992); Chrystos, *Not Vanishing, Dream On, In Her I Am* (Vancouver: Press Gang, 1988, 1991, 1993); Janice Gould, *Beneath My Heart* (Ithaca: Firebrand, 1990).

The use of erotic imaging in Native lesbian work becomes a tool by which we heal ourselves. This tool is powerfully and deftly evident in the hands of these writers, especially the poems of Janice Gould and Chrystos. In my own work, I have explored such themes as self-lovemaking, and the act of love between two women[20] as a way to mend the broken circles of my own life, and hopefully to give sustenance to other woman who are searching for new maps for their lives. But Native lesbian writing is not only about sex and/or sexuality. There is a broader cultural definition of sexuality that is at work here. Strong bonds to Earth and Her inhabitants serve as a pivotal edge to our most sensual writing. Like our heterosexual sisters, Native lesbians who write are swift to call out the oppressions that are at work in our lives. Homophobia is the eldest son of racism; they work in concert with each other, whether externally or internally. Native lesbian writing *names* those twin evils that would cause destruction to us.

A major theme in the work of Vickie Sears, Cherokee Nation, is the power over children's bodies by the State.[21] Sexual abuse, physical abuse, emotional abuse are "normal" occurrences to the girl-children in Vickie's short stories. Herself a survivor of the foster-care system, Sears finds her solace and empowerment through the things of Earth and the love between women. Her short stories emphasize these possibilities of self-recovery. Indeed, one could say that much of Native lesbian writing celebrates Earth as woman, as lover, as companion. Woman, lover, companion celebrated as Earth. Two-Spirit writers are merging the selves that colonialism splits apart.

Recovery writing is another component in the movement of Native women writers. Recovery from substance abuse, as well as racism, sexism and homophobia. Two Feathers, Cayuga Nation, is a wonderful example of this kind of recovery writing, as is Sharon Day of the Ojibway Nation.[22] Again, Chrystos, Menominee poet, excels

---

20 Beth Brant, *Mohawk Trail* (Ithaca: Firebrand, 1985; Toronto Women's Press, 1990); Beth Brant, *Food & Spirits* (Vancouver: Press Gang, 1991).

21 Vickie Sears, *Simple Songs* (Ithaca: Firebrand, 1990).

22 Sharon Day and Two Feathers, unpublished manuscripts.

in the naming of what it feels like to be hooked and in thrall to the substances that deaden the pain of being Native in the 20th century. Highly charged with anger, this recovery-writing is, at the same time, gentle with the knowing of how difficult the path is toward the Good Red Road. There is empathy and compassion in the telling of our people's struggle to stay clean and sober, there is rage against the State that employed *and* employs addiction to attempt our cultural annihilation. Many of my short stories focus on that moment between staying sober and taking "just one" drink. The characters are caught in that timescape of traditional Native "seeing," and the unnatural landscape of colonization through addiction. In my stories, as in my life, Creator brings gifts of the natural to "speak" to these characters. It then becomes a choice to live on the Good Red Road, or to die the death of being out of balance—a kind of "virtual reality," as opposed to the real, the natural.

Pauline Johnson knew firsthand the effects of these attempts at annihilation. Her father, a Chief of the Mohawk Nation, was a political activist against the rum-runners who would have weakened his people. Severely beaten many times by these smugglers and murderers, his life was considerably shortened. Many of Pauline's stories are filled with righteous anger against the whiteman who wished to rape our land, using alcohol as a weapon to confuse and subjugate us. I think she would applaud the recovery-writing and name it for what it is—an Indian war cry against the assassination of our culture.

Oral tradition requires a telling and a listening that is intense, and intentional. Giving, receiving, giving—it makes a complete circle of Indigenous truth. First Nations writing utilizes the power and gift of story, like oral tradition, to convey history, lessons, culture and spirit. And perhaps the overwhelming instinct in our spirit is to love. I would say that Native writing gives the gift of love. And love is a word that is abused and made empty by the dominant culture. In fact, the letters l-o-v-e have become just that, blank cyphers used frivolously to cover up deep places of the spirit.

I began writing when I turned forty. I imagine the spirits knew I wasn't ready to receive that gift until I was mature enough and open enough to understand the natural meaning of love. I believe that the writing being created by First Nations women is writing done with a community consciousness. Individuality is a concept and philosophy that has little meaning for us. Even while being torn from our spiritual places of home, having our ancestors names stolen and used to sell sports teams, automobiles, or articles of clothing; having our languages beaten out of us through residential school systems even while having our spirits defiled and blasphemed, our families torn apart by institutionalized violence and genocide, even after this long war, we still remain connected to our own.

Our connections take many forms. I, as a Mohawk, feel deep spiritual bonds towards many who do not come from my Nation. These people, Carrier, Menominee, Cree, Cherokee, Lakota, Inuit, Abenaki and many others, are like the threads of a weaving. This Mohawk and the people of many Nations are warp and woof to each other. While the colour and beauty of each thread is unique and important, together they make a communal material of strength and durability. Such is our writing, because such is our belief-system. Writing is an act that can take place in physical isolation, but the memory of history, of culture, of land, of Nation, is always present—like another being. That is how we create. Writing with all our senses, and with the ones that have not been named or colonized, we create.

Janice Gould, Maidu Nation, has written, "I would like to believe there are vast reserves of silences that can never be *forced* to speak, that remain sacred and safe from violation."[23] I feel that these sacred silences are the place *from* which we write. That place that has not been touched or stained by imperialism and hatred. That sacred place. That place.

Like Pauline Johnson, mixed-blood writers find those sacred places in the blood that courses through our bodies, whispering, "come home, come home." Although we have never left that home, in a sense we have been pulled and pushed into accepting the lies told about our Indian selves. For those of us who do not conform to a stereotype of what Native people "look like," claiming our identities as Native people becomes an exercise in racism: "Gee,

23 Janice Gould, "Disobedience in Language: Texts by Lesbian Natives" (Speech to the Modern Language Association, New York, 1990).

you don't look like an Indian." "Gee, I didn't know Indians had blue eyes." "My great great-grandmother was a Cherokee princess, does that make me an Indian too?" After a while it almost becomes humourous, even as it's tiresome. Perhaps the feeling is that we're getting away with something, that we are tapping into unknown strengths, for which we are not entitled. And how the dominant culture loves to quantify suffering and pain! And how well it has worked to divide us from each other and from our self. Colourism is another force of racism. And we write about that, exposing our fears of abandonment by the people we love, the people whose opinion matters, the very people who, in our dreams, whisper, "Come home, come home." Yet, mixed-blood writing is also what I have been examining; for most of us are bloods of many mixes and Nations. Linda Hogan, Chickasaw Nation calls us "New People." New People are the survivors of five hundred years of colonial rule. Our grandmothers' bodies were appropriated by the conquerors, but the New People have not forgotten that grandmother, nor the legacy she carried in her womb.

In Mexico, a story is told of La Llorona. It is told that she wanders throughout the land, looking for her lost children. Her voice is the wind. She weeps and moans and calls to the children of her blood. She is the Indian, the mother of our blood, the grandmother of our hearts. She calls to us. "Come home, come home," she whispers, she cries, she calls to us. She comes into that sacred place we hold inviolate. She is birthing us in that sacred place. "Come home, come home," the voice of the umbilical, the whisper of the placenta. "Come home, come home." We listen. And we write.

Anodynes and Amulets

We are surrounded by magazines, journals and idiom of the New Age religion. This religion has no specific dogma or doctrine other than heavy reliance on paraphernalia and language, some of it "borrowed" from Indigenous cultures. In one magazine, a shamanic tour is offered, for which a person may spend several thousands of dollars to travel to holy places of spirit with an "experienced" shaman. Supposedly the end result will be communication with whatever spirits choose to present themselves to the pilgrims. Aside from the obvious distress to land that will be travelled upon, trampled upon, there is the arrogance and blasphemy implied by the belief that spirits will come at the bidding of pilgrims who have money to buy them. I realize this is a basic tenet of christianity, especially the Catholic church, but it seems that those folks who are anxious to have an experience with *otherworldly* beings are the same people who would declare they are colour-blind or refer to Indigenous peoples of any continent as "our Natives." There is the same kind of patronizing and ethnocentric behavior being acted out as that of the missionary and the liberal.

In another journal, an interview with a "channeller" is displayed. A channeller is a person who is taken over by the spirit of another and who speaks with the other's voice. Channellers come in both sexes—bleached blonde woman in Chicago channels a South Asian man, named Ramtha, who lived many centuries ago. A pale, bland man is channelling the voice of the archangel Michael. All channellers are white. I am reminded of a letter Linda Hogan received from a white woman who claimed she channeled the spirit of a dolphin, and therefore also laid claim to being a "sister" to Linda. Linda was bemused by both claims. She guessed the channeller assumed that Indians did this activity all the time and would welcome a non-Indian into the ranks of our Nations. But as Linda said to me, "What self-respecting Dolphin would speak *to* her [the woman who wrote the letter], much less *through* her?" We laughed together over this latest attempt to colonize our belief systems, but under the laughter was anger. It's not enough that they appropriate *us*, they also want to subsume the spirit of all living things.

In these magazines are advertisements for computer astral charts, books on metaphysical subjects and shamans, books on Hindu and Buddhist masters, books chronicling the spirit-chasers' adventures on aboriginal lands. There books about white people taken aboard alien ships, then returning to earth at the astonishment and confusion of their families and neighbours, ultimately acquiring agents to hawk their stories to publishers and movie producers. There are advertisements for weekends of spiritual harmony with whomever is a popular practitioner at the time. Even has-been actors, hoping to shore up their waning bank accounts and visibility, have become groupies or shills for these practitioners. I assume their jobs are to lend some show biz glamour to a dull act!

There are all-women and all-men retreats. The women are supposed to get in touch with the goddess within. The men are supposed to get in touch with their fathers and their maleness. Of course, male or female, drumming and dancing are required, feathers are worn, "names" are given, lots of hugging and getting in touch with feelings. O Capitalism, how mighty art thou! For thousands of dollars, thee will give something to fill the aching hearts and souls of a bereft society.

There are crystals everywhere. Advertised in new-age magazines, in feminist journals, in catalogues. The mining of these stones has caused a depletion and collapse of old caves and caverns, especially in parts of South America. I guess it has not occurred to consumers and salesmen that the reason there *are* special places that resonate are because the stones were *there*, not hanging around the necks of gullible and weary pilgrims who quest for some anodyne to a cold and loveless society.

I cannot document when this movement started to gain force. In reading the many newspapers and magazines, one might come to the conclusion that the new-age religion is a natural phenomenon that had come into being as a resistance to materialism and conspicuous consumption of goods and services. It would seem that people had lost ties to a spiritual base. But I am talking about white people, because in all the information I have gathered, this religion and/or movement is populated by Anglos and most especially, Anglos with money to spend. This is not a "free" or inexpensive religion. If you want it bad enough, you have to pay. How can a spiritual base be bought? How can a spirit be called with money? But there it is—you pay your money, you get *it*. The new-age is merely the old-age—capitalism cloaked in mystic terminology, dressed in robes and skins of ancient and Indigenous beliefs. This is all so familiar to me. The Blackrobes with their cross and rum proclaimed a new age for Indigenous peoples. The Spanish, the French, the British, the Dutch proclaimed a new world for themselves. And while the colonialists appropriated land and bodies, the new-age appropriates belief and turns it to their own use. This religion is the colonizing of spirit *and* spirits.

If the new-age religion is a resistance to materialism, where is the resistance? If it is a movement, where is it moving to? Nowhere do I see the formation of a catalyst that challenges the existence of the status quo. What I do see are bits and pieces of this and that to improve individual life. What kind of movement is it that only encompasses an individual lifestyle? Where is community in this religion/movement?

In all the propaganda of the new-age I've read, there is no mention of lesbians or gay men. This is not surprising in itself; the surprise comes when I see so many gay men and lesbians following this religion. I am especially disheartened by the new-age making inroads into the lives of people who are HIV positive or have AIDS. While I fully believe that people have choices and the desire to be comforted in times of sorrow and travail is universal, a popular belief amongst new-agers is that we have chosen our destinies and illnesses. In other words, my friends "chose" to get AIDS and die painfully and horribly. This sounds like fundamental christianity to me. If we were all straight and white, in other words, "good," we wouldn't have nearly the trouble we are having. And if we've "chosen" to be of colour, we better soon discover our place, catering to the whims of the white populace that wants what they think we have—a mysterious communication with spirits that the whiteman can't see or hear.

If I didn't know how insidious racism can be and how it is wrapped in the arms and legs of the institutions of state, church and media, I would feel great compassion for the pilgrims of the new religion. To be honest, I do feel a pity for them. Is no one happy? Is no one at peace? And yet, my pity does not render me incapable of challenging the emptiness of the dominant culture's belief system. There *is* no belief, except in that of money and power over. This belief has spilled into my communities. There are Native "plastic shamans" who do sweats, who give workshops, who sell tapes to hungry white souls. And I find this as unforgivable and blasphemous as I do a Lynn Andrews who writes lies and sells those lies.

The new-age religion is so ethereal. Ethereality is light and wispy. Earth and Her creatures are not. A tree is sturdy, sheds leaves, turns colour, exhibits cycles of regeneration. A stone is quiet, finds its way into water or earth. A bull moose moves through forest, munching on green things, growing antlers, rutting in a noisy, community ritual. These are the physical evidences of spirituality in my belief system. So is sexual activity, laughing, making soup, taking a bath, having a menstrual cycle, taking my grandchildren to see turtles. Perhaps it is solidity of Native beliefs that are so attractive to white people who grew up on a diet of christian miracles. But belief in Earth and Her magic is just not "mystical" or "ethereal" enough for people who seem to need a more colourful and packaged product in which to invest.

Leslie Silko, when asked by a white woman how to learn about Indian religions, replied, "Get involved in environmental issues. Help save Earth from destruction. This is our religion." However, I think Leslie knew, as I do, that her reply was not what the white woman wanted to hear. She wanted to hear of ceremony, of ritual, of gods and goddesses, of secret societies, of secrets. And those who want to invest in our spirituality do not want to hear that we would sometimes like to have their presence when we are trying to protect our land and culture; that sometimes it would be useful to hear their voices raised in protest when our land and culture are being threatened. The ethos of the new-age is passivity and dilettantism.

I am distressed at attempts of the women's movement to appropriate symbols and history of other cultures and renaming that "women's culture" or "lesbian culture." One can only come from one's own culture and class. We are not born full-blown into feminists or lesbians. We come from families, from communities, from religions, from Nations that inform us as human beings. It may be possible to discard or put away those values that reek of racism, sexism, and homophobia, but we can't remake ourselves into an image that is just another take on a racist formula. I am incensed when white feminists want to insist that Native religions have goddess figures. That is a European concept and has no place in our beliefs. The same holds true of wicce or witchcraft. Mohawk Got'go' is *not* to be defined by European models. It is difficult to exorcise the predominance of the English language, but it is possible to understand that although we may share a common language, *my* definition is not necessarily one that is parallel to that of a Euro-christian culture.

Arrogance that exhibits itself through language, through ethnocentrism is a hallmark of the new-age. The belief that human beings are more important than any other part of Creation. The belief that holy places and holy beings are defined by capitalism. I once wrote a poem, years ago, about many old women gathered together to perform a ceremony. The "ceremony" was a celebration of the ordinary—a bird's feather, a cradleboard, a beaver skin. I was amazed that many white people asked me if this was a "real" ceremony, a genuine Mohawk ritual. Amazed, because they misunderstood the whole essence behind the words. No, this was not a "real" ceremony; I wouldn't describe or write about a religious event that takes place in my community. But this poem was my attempt at sharing what is holy to me, the magic of things that are common and useful. That the commonness of a bird's feather is precisely what makes it magic. That mystery is fused with the everyday. That Beaver once wore this skin and her spirit lives in the warm fur. That when a Turtle rattle is shaken, that *is* the voice of Turtle. That laughter accompanies spiritual celebrations. That old women touch and value each other. I was struck by the sad inability of some to see the elemental, physical, sensuous foundation of my belief. They would rather have been privy to some "exotic" ritual than to accept a gift from me. They saw a pretty package, but were unaware of what it contained, because it was impossible for them to believe that a bird's feather is as valuable as the human holding it.

To the new-ager, a superficial feeding of the bare spots of the heart is what is seen as important. I call this racism because underneath the questing is really the belief that they are superior and only need to partake of certain magics to uphold the fallacy that they are dispensing largesse to the great unwashed and uncultured. In other words, the new-age is doing Indigenous peoples a favour by stealing our ceremony and ritual. Does this sound familiar? Isn't this what the christian churches have done for centuries and continue to do?

The similarities between christianity and new-age religion are exhibited in the certainty that *their* way is *the* way. Collecting monies and souls, dispensing amulets and anodynes (for a price), and telling the non-believers that the path to fulfilment is paved with money—the seeker's money, that is. I think a channeller would be perfectly comfortable in Vatican City. And the Pope would feel at home in the luxurious surroundings of Ramtha's house.

Now, I may be giving the impression that I *am* an intolerant, hateful woman. I am not. I am an angry woman. And a sad woman. What on Earth can heal all those broken people who sincerely look for alternative ways to find wholeness? I don't know, but I will suggest activism. I will suggest political involvement in issues that threaten land and peoples. I realize this holds no glamour or reward. But I am also much more concerned with what can heal the broken Nations of my people.

I remember a concert I attended years and years ago. Chris Williamson (a white feminist singer) was performing. She was talking about Leonard Peltier and his incarceration for a crime that he didn't commit. Her speech was going along fine until she made the statement that "everyone" should get to know a Native American. "It will make your life richer." As if we were placed on Earth to enrich white people's lives! As if we stood around on corners, hoping to be picked up by white people so they can have an "experience." We *have* enriched white people's lives. Natives and people of colour have worked someone else's farms, have raised white babies, have coddled and cajoled white men, have made life easier for white women by providing domestic work, have cooked food for white stomachs while going hungry ourselves, have fought in their armies for their never-ending wars. Yes, we have made their lives richer, and continue to do so as they appropriate our spirituality. None of this was given. It was taken. And I find this fascination with and practice of Indigenous religions a rape.

First Nations people are seen as a stereotype. There is no thought to the fact that we work, we play, we worry, we make love. There is no thought that our Elders like gossip or Bingo. There is no thought that we rush off to catch planes, write poetry, wash clothes, walk picket lines, put cars together. The new-age does not see us in our human spectrum. It is easier and less complicated for them to view us as artifacts or symbols that are waiting to be scooped up, inspected, *used* as they see fit.

There is no doubt that we see the universe through a different set of values and beliefs. It is impossible for non-Natives to *feel* the sorts of emotions that are called upon when Indigenous peoples speak about ancestors, about Earth, about the symbiosis that exists between human and animal. Non-Natives come from another psychic and physical place. *We* have been here for centuries. Our ritual has meaning because we are *from here,* not because we plucked it out of the air and thought it would be fun or nice to perform. It is in us, perhaps even in the DNA of our cells, to give ourselves over to what whispers to us from the corn, from Deer, from Heron, from the rock that resides on the bottom of the waters. We have a relationship with the beings who share Earth with us.

I believe that non-Natives can love the wild spices can feel the excitement of Cranes lifting off into sky, can testify to the beauty that still lives abundantly in North America. I believe this, for I have heard it expressed and written about. I also know that *our* love comes from a commitment to Earth; She is our Mother, She holds the bones of our ancestors in trust. The very trees hold our stories. Our spirits hover and gather around us. We know the words to use to bring them closer, to intervene for us.

I long for a conclusion to the new-age religion, and in its place, a healthy respect for sovereignty and the culture that makes Nationhood. We do not object to non-Natives praying *with* us (if invited). We object to the theft of our prayers that have no psychic meaning to them. Our belief systems contain the cosmos of history and regeneration, of harmonious and balanced thought that has travelled on this land, touching Aboriginal mind, intertwining with beings who live alongside us. This cannot be bought with capitalistic or colonial greed. It is ours. We have always been generous peoples, giving food and knowledge to those who visited us. But what is in our blood is neither for sale nor for a fast spiritual fix. If non-Natives are hungry, let them learn to make food from what is in *their* blood.

Recovery and Transformation[1]

Last weekend in Minneapolis was the first gathering of gay and lesbian Two-Spirits—The Basket and the Bow.[2] This gathering was a joyful one, a reunion of sorts—much like a pow wow, where we go to see old friends, share stories with family, catch up on tribal happenings, take care of Indigenous business—the difference being that this reunion was largely between people who had never met.

Cree, Ojibway, Mohawk, Athabascan, Paiute, Lakota, Metis; so many Nations represented by our Queer citizens. Our initial shyness soon was dispelled by our great happiness in being with each other. *Us*, our family.

We talked, we laughed, we wept together. We told our stories, we listened, we touched. And as I talked with my sisters and brothers and listened, listened to the voices telling their lives, two words kept insisting their message onto my brain.

Recovery. Transformation.

Recovery. Transformation.

Recovery is the act of taking control over the forces that would destroy us. Recovery from alcohol and drug use—most definitely. But another kind of recovery is taking place in our family. Recovery from the disease of homophobia. This disease has devastated my Indian family as surely as smallpox, alcohol, glue-sniffing and tuberculosis have devastated our Nations. Recovery is not an act that ignores the disease. Recovery is becoming *stronger* than the disease. The evidence was there before my eyes. For two days we

---

1   Speech given at the National Women's Studies Conference, Minneapolis, Minnesota, 1988.

2   The Basket and Bow gathering took place June 18-19, 1988 in Minneapolis, Minnesota. The title of the gathering comes from an Ojibwe story that tells of an Elder giving a child the choice of which path to follow. Some girlchildren selected the basket. Some boychildren selected the bow. And some girls and boys chose both, claiming the two-spirited path as the one they would follow. This story was related to me by Sharon Day.

assured each other that we won't self-destruct any more, we won't be shamed any more, *we won't go away.*

We come from an ancient tradition. Our languages, sabotaged by outsiders for almost five hundred years, all contain words for us.[3] The exorcisms that the christian church has conducted over us have not worked. Yet, we are in mourning for all those who came before us and are to follow, those who did not and do not *know* that we are many, and that we have formed battalions to fight this disease. We ask the questions: How many of our teen-age brothers and sisters commit suicide because they think they are alone in their gayness? Can these suicides only be defined as despair over living in poverty and a lost culture? Who will dare to ask these questions if not us?

Transformation. The act of changing the function or condition of. We begin by changing the internalization of homophobia into a journey of healing. There is a coming-clean that takes place on this journey. We cleanse ourselves according to our spiritual beliefs and world-views. Albert told a story of when he felt ready to participate in the Sun Dance, but was fearful of transphobic reaction. He went to a Medicine Woman who told him, "You will present yourself to Creator, not the people." Albert took this message to his heart. A Sun Dance can last hours or days, until a communion with Creator is made. Albert made this communion and presented himself with a full knowledge of who he is and what he is to his community. I like that phrase, *present yourself.* It seems to fit us so much better than *coming out.*

On our separate, yet communal journeys, we have learned that a hegemonic gay and lesbian movement cannot encompass our complicated history—history that involves so much loss. Nor can a hegemonic gay and lesbian movement give us tools to heal our broken Nations. But our strength as a family not only gives tools, it helps *make* tools.

---

3 Nadle, shopan, a-go-kwa, ayekkewe, bade, winkte, geenumu gesallagee, ma ai, pote are words in Navajo, Aleut, Chippewa, Cree, Crow, Lakota, MicMac, Shoshone respectively, that are still in use. See also, Maurice Kenny, "Tinselled Bucks;" Will Rosco, ed., Living the Spirit (New York: St. Martin's Press, 1988); and Walter Williams, The Spirit in the Flesh (Boston: Beacon Press, 1986).

Presenting ourselves to the Creator means realigning ourselves within our communities and within our spiritual selves to create balance. Balance will keep us whole. To be a First Nations Two-Spirit means to be on a path that won't be blocked by anyone or anything. To be an Indian lesbian or gay man at this time means that a woman like me won't have to search and re-search for the Barbara Camerons to keep me sane and unafraid.[4] The Barbara Camerons of the future are here in the printed word, on the tapes, on film, on this stage, in this audience. There will be no cover-up in this recovery—by white imperialism or by my own people. There are too many of us now. We are too savvy, too knowledgeable of the colonialist's mind, too well-versed in our politics to allow ourselves to be hidden again under the layers of anthropological bullshit, or through denial, or the looks of anger that come from our heterosexual brothers' and sisters' eyes.

If our existence can be denied, then so can the existence of infant mortality or the chipping away of our lands, stone by stone. If you believe in the existence of wild rice, blue herons, the moon—you have to believe in us. For we are part of all that exists.

Recovery means that we transform ourselves. Presenting ourselves means that we transform our world. This has been made so clear. Many of us are substance-abuse counsellors, lawyers skilled in sovereignty issues. We are health care workers, teachers, midwives, artists, actors, writers, mothers, fathers, lovers. Our political acts—and our very survival *is* a political act—are transforming the face of Indian Country and marking roads into the heart of North America.

There is a personal recovery taking place in me. For the last two years I have been on a journey of physical illness, culminating in a small stroke and a ten hour surgery to bypass a congenital condition in my femoral artery that had almost stopped the flow of blood to my legs. This journey took many turnings I would not have chosen

---

4   Barbara Cameron is the co-founder of Gay American Indians. Founded in the early seventies, GAI has been a resource for all Native Two-Spirits who think they are alone. The organization is based in San Francisco. Barbara Cameron has been an inspiration to all Native lesbians. Writer, activist, mother, freedom fighter, she worked for all of us, and gave us courage to keep going.

for myself, such as the incredible pain when I walked even a few feet. And this pain also clouded my emotional being, my spiritual being. I began to distrust people who loved me. I was unkind to those who would have helped me. And I was unkindest to myself and gave up the thing that I loved—writing. I welcomed my oldest "friend" —self-hatred.

As the stroke was beginning in my arms, travelling to my right leg, then moving up to my face, I shouted "NO!" The echoes of that *no* bounced around in my ears. Terrified and almost incapable of thought or action, the words *not yet, not yet, not yet,* were sounding like a drum with each heart's beat. Later in the hospital I thought about the arrogance of those words, *not yet.* I, who had forgotten the joy of life, had the fear of losing it.

When I came home after the long days of healing, I wanted to celebrate the rejuvenation of my body and spirit by making love. Denise was fearful of hurting me, but I persisted, feeling that sex was another kind of beginning for me, because this too was something I had denied myself. My participation in such a primal ritual was an important component in my wellness.

I have thought about the transformative power of sexuality. The *magic* of sex that has been trivialized by a dominant and empty society. *Our* sexuality is despised because sex is despised, unless shrouded in misogynist and/or racist winding sheets. That sad, dominant society that embraces death even as it fears it, does not understand that recovery is transformation, and transformation is an act of love. But we have always known that acts of love are the very reason we are here.

Lesbian and gay Natives will become and are becoming the Elders of our people, giving counsel and wisdom. We are presenting ourselves in the fullest way possible for us. This can only be a good thing for our communities. Because we do not search for ourselves alone, as individuals. It is a community effort. I have always thought that Native people bring a particular kind of beauty to this world. Lesbian and gay Natives expand that beauty by bringing our transformative love to those who would receive it—our people.

Nia:wen.

From the Inside—Looking at You[1]

The title of this workshop, "From the Outside Looking In," implies that those of us on this panel are somehow on the outside of the normal, the real and the truth. I must protest this abrogation of our thoughts and words to fit a white-defined framework of what constitutes racism and writing. As a Mohawk, I am very much inside my own world-view, my own Nation, and I am looking at you—the descendants of the European fathers who colonized that world.

My people are an oral people. This means that our stories, our history, our value-systems, our spirituality have been given to us by the spoken, not the written word. And because our words were spoken, it is important that we choose words carefully, and that we *listen* with equal care. I want you to know this because as a Native woman who writes, as well as speaks, I feel a great responsibility to share words that are truthful. I have heard non-Natives say that truth is a "relative thing." We do not believe in that philosophy. Indeed, that philosophy has been a force behind the onslaught of colonization.

During the physical and cultural genocide perpetrated upon my people, the Europeans came with a book, and that book was called the holy bible. Through the use and enforcement of that book, those written words, everything that *we* had known was shattered. Our world was splintered, and we are left with the excruciating task of finding the pieces of our world and making it right again, making it balanced again. For this is at the heart of our search—restoring balance within our communities in a dominant culture that has gone amok with greed and worship of individualism. What does this have to do with racism and writing? Everything.

Literacy is a new concept to us, the Indigenous peoples of North America. As of today, 50 percent of my people are either illiterate

---

1 From a panel entitled "From the Outside Looking In: Racism and Writing," given at the Gay Games Literary Festival: Crossing Borders, Vancouver, B.C., 1990.

or functionally literate (by western standards). We do not have the seeming luxury of research. We cannot go to a book and find out who was gay or lesbian, who said this at time, who said that at what time—for books, like the bible, are distortions of the truth—starting with the Jesuits and continuing with modern-day "priests" like Grey Owl, Lynn Andrews and Tony Hillermon. We must rely on memory, our Elders, our collective dreams to find those pieces that were cut from us. The written word, the bible book almost destroyed our faith in who we are, and so we have come to view the written word with suspicion and apprehension. The lies about us in the form of letters, sentences, paragraphs proliferate like a virus and spread negation and invisibility. "Indian experts" are inevitably white men and women who presume to do the talking for us as if we are a dead people.[2] But, you get the picture, poor, dead Indians, with no one to speak on our behalf except for the liberal whiteman. When it comes to "folk-tales" or "myths," they scour the continent for "genuine" Natives. But it also seems that we have had the last laugh in the circus of anthro-gladiators. Our Elders have told us that many so-called informants deliberately gave wrong information to the anthros. An Indian joke, folks!

Those of us who are Native and have *chosen* to write are a fast-growing community. This has not been an easy path to travel. For myself, this entails being in a constant state of translation. Those of you for whom English is a second language will understand some of what I say. Not only am I translating from the spoken to the written, but also writing in a language that is not my own. When I sit in front of my typewriter, there are times I literally cannot find the words that will describe what I want to say. And that is because the words I want, the words I "hear," are Mohawk words. But you see, my Mohawk language was virtually destroyed in my family. My grandmother and grandfather were taught, in residential school, that Mohawk was a bad thing. To speak Mohawk, to be Mohawk. After hundreds of years of emotional and physical assault on us

---

2 A notable exception is Richard Drinnon's *Facing West: The Metaphysics of Indian Hating and Empire Building* (Minneapolis, MN: University of Minnesota Press, 1980), an excellent analysis of racism from the "wild west" to the jungles of Vietnam. This book has been sadly neglected in favour of more palatable books on the "plight" of the Indian.

for using the language Creator gave us, we now find it in our best interests to communicate with the language the enemy forced on us. Therefore, I bend and shape this unlovely language in a way that will make truth. Because the language of the enemy was a weapon used to perpetuate racism and hate, I want to forge it in a new way, as a weapon of love. I also feel that a piece of writing is not finished until it is spoken. I read my work aloud as I write, after I write and often when I am sleeping. My stories are *meant* to be spoken. My work is *meant* to be said out loud. In sign or by voice, storytelling is a natural act. I also feel that I must say this—I do not write for you who are white. I write for my own. Another natural act.

This leads me to ask you who are white to listen to us, the Aboriginal peoples whose land you occupy. What you will hear from us is the truth of how it is with us. The truth does not lie in the realm of colonial supremacy, nor in the kingdom of imperialistic propaganda. No one can speak for us but us. There may be those of European descent who want to be our allies in the elimination of racism. I welcome you. My people welcome you. Dionne Brand has said that if a white writer introduces a character of colour into their writings, that writer must be accountable for his or her place in that writing.[3] Why do you write about a person of colour? This is an important question, but the answer is even more so, since our history of the last five hundred years is so entangled with yours. I do not say that only Native peoples can write about Natives. I will never say that. I do say that you can't steal my story and call it your own. You can't steal my spirit and call it yours. This has been the North American Dream—stolen land, stolen children, stolen lives, stolen dreams—and now we are *all* living the nightmare of this thievery. If your history is one of cultural dominance, you must be aware of and *own* that history before you can write about me and mine. This can be liberating for you. I'm sure there are many in this audience who are recovering from alcohol, drug and food addictions. Racism is also an addiction, one from which it is possible to recover. There

---

3 Yet another panel on "Racism and Writing." This one took place at West Words, a writing workshop for women held every year in Vancouver, B.C. Dionne spoke eloquently to the subject.

are no Twelve-Step programs for this one, however. This recovery is a solitary one, even with support.

Those of us who are Native have internalized the racism that devastated our lands like biological warfare. For some, this is reason enough why we don't or can't write. For centuries we have heard the words used to describe us: dumb Indian, lazy Indian, ugly Indian, drunken Indian, crazy Indian. It has been nearly impossible to not have these messages encoded on our brains. Messages that play back in our heads whenever we step outside "our place." Messages that still proliferate from the media, from the institutions, from the christian church. To write or not to write is a painful struggle for us. Everything we write can be used against us. *Everything we write will be used against us.* And I'm not talking about bad reviews. I'm talking about the flak we receive from our own communities as well as the smug liberalism from the white, "literary" enclave.

Writing is an act of courage for most. For *us*, it is an act that requires opening up our wounded communities, our families, to eyes and ears that do not love us. Is this madness? In a way it is— the madness of a Louis Riel, a Maria Campbell, a Pauline Johnson, a Crazy Horse—a revolutionary madness. A love that is greater than fear. A love that is as tender as it is fierce. Writing is also a gift. For me, it is a precious gift given to me in my fortieth year of life on Earth. Along with the gift came instruction to use this gift on behalf of love.

I feel a personal responsibility and a strong desire to tell the truth. Sometimes that desire is a physical craving as I sit in front of my machine, sweating, hurting, struggling with a *contra* language to conceive new words. I desire to make rage a living testament. I desire to heal. I desire to make beauty out of circumstances that are not beautiful. I desire truth.

I also want to share this desire. I want allies and lovers in this war against racism. I want honesty from allies and lovers. I want acts of love to be committed in all our languages.

It is said that the Mohawk language was first spoken by a woman, and it became her responsibility to teach all who came from her womb. Racism and homophobia were unknown words to her and her descendants. I have also heard and dreamed that her first words were those of thanks—thanks for the paradise that was entrusted to her care and respect—a trust that has been handed down story after story after story. The carriers of the bible book brought a new kind of story to us, a story that resounds with cacophony and cruelty. We are holding on to what is still intact— our spirit, our strength. And when I use the enemy's language to hold onto my strength as a Mohawk lesbian writer, I use it as my own instrument of power in this long, long battle against racism.

Nai:wen.

Physical Prayers

I was told a story.[1] On feast days, after the food was eaten, after the dancing, after the singing prayers, another kind of prayer was begun. Men and women chose who they wished to be partnered with, retired to places on open ground, and commenced the ritual of love-making. As the touching, stroking and special play was being enacted, and the sighs and cries were filling the air, the spirit of each individual became a communal prayer of thanksgiving. Sexuality, and the magic ability of our bodies to produce orgasm was another way to please Creator and ensure all was well and in balance in our world.

As a creative human being who is also Native and Two-Spirit, I will not make distinctions between sexuality and spirituality. To separate them would mean to place these two words in competition with each other, to rate them in acquiescence to white-European thought, to deny the power of sex/spirit in my life, my work.

In white North America, sex and spiritual beliefs are commodities, packaged and sold in the markets of free enterprise. From the golden halls of Vatican City to the strychnine-laced paths of Jonestown, the story is the same: confine the minds and bodies of the followers, especially the minds and bodies of those who are poor and of colour, and make sure the women answer to only one person—a white male who can rape at will, who can dole out forgiveness and redemption for a price, who decides which life is expendable and which is not. The emperors of free enterprise claim belief in god and family. Yet, I believe at the root of their belief-system is a hatred of sex. A people who despise sex must also despise their god. Why else do they make a vast chasm between the two? Does their attempt to make both god and sex into images

---

1 In a conversation with Donna Marchand, Native lesbian writer and student of law, Donna brought up the concept of orgasm as a natural resource. I thank her most gratefully for the brilliance of her mind.

that fit a white-male thesis (christianity) mean that they will like themselves more?

As a lesbian, I know that the dominant culture only sees me as a sexually uninhibited creature. As a Native lesbian, I know that the dominant culture does not see me at all, or sees an aberration of a "dead" culture. By daring to love and have sex with another like myself, I have stepped beyond any boundary the emperors could have imagined. In the emperors' eyes, sexual freedom means freedom from *them*, a scary thought to be sure. There is no money to be made from the likes of me, except from the porn trade, and even then, lesbian lovemaking is just a prelude to the "real" thing—penetration by a man.

I became a lesbian in my thirty-third year of life. I had crushes on girls as a youth, and even had a sexual encounter at the age of sixteen with an older woman of eighteen who asked if she could eat my cherry. Of course I said yes! Curiosity, desire, longing to break any rules, I let my cherry be eaten and look back on that moment with a sweet nostalgia. I don't know if I was born a lesbian, and I don't care. I find the recent preoccupation with nature vs. nurture very tiresome and dangerous. In my thirty-third year of life I was a feminist, an activist and largely occupied with discovering all things female. And one of those lovely discoveries was that I could love women sexually, emotionally, and spiritually—and all at once. This is why I choose to be lesbian. It makes me more complete in myself, and a whole woman is of much better use to my communities than a split one. Now, in my fifty-third year of life I am a feminist, an activist and a grandmother and still in the early stages of discovery and wisdom. But I do think of that distant moment when an older woman of eighteen gave me such pleasure and allowed me to know my body's desires. I am not one who wonders, "What if?" yet I am fairly certain that if I had followed my inclination, I may have become that older woman's "lady," and perhaps would have slipped easily into the gay life of the 50s. I was/am very much a child of my class—I would have gotten a job cashiering or as a saleslady, my lover would have worked on the line, and we would have made a home in a fairly traditional butch/femme way; I probably never would have become a writer, much less a woman who says the word lesbian out loud in front of strangers! And my being Native, being Mohawk, might have been a source of distant amusement or puzzlement to my lover. We would have been women of our time and class. I expect my family would have reacted in much the same way they did years later—accepting a white woman into the family because I loved her. But our lives would have been hidden from the dominant culture.

The blending of Native and lesbian, which to men, has been a sensual and pleasing journey, is not so pleasant to some of my own Native sisters and brothers of the heterosexual persuasion. I could discount their anger, and/or off-handedly blame colonialism (which is to blame), but I desire to look further into the heart of this anger and imagine a revelation that could possibly transform us as individuals and community members. This is something I cannot do alone.

I don't know if all First Nations had words or expressions to connote their Two-Spirit members. I cannot find a word in Mohawk that describes me, however, Mohawk is a woman language; if gender is not described in other terms, it is assumed to be female. Perhaps a Two-Spirit was not an *uncommon* enough occurrence to be granted a special word. And perhaps a gay man was known by a female term, and a lesbian like myself was a woman among many other women. I *am* certain that I am not the first Mohawk lesbian to walk this Earth, and that certainty has helped ease the pain I feel when confronted by another Native who discounts me because of my sexuality. I also don't know if all First Spirits gave special or exalted status to their Two-Spirit citizens. There are some stories of Two-Spirits being revered *because* of their blurred gender and uncompromising way of living within their clan or tribal unit.[2] These stories are important ones to treasure and repeat to our young, but I think they cannot take the place of living and breathing lesbians and gay men who can be role models if we are able to jump over the chasm that homophobia has blasted into our Nations. And many of us find ourselves at the edge of this precipice separating us from our beloved people.

---

2 See Will Roscoe, *The Zuni Man-Woman* (Albuquerque: University of New Mexico Press, 1991).

Those first whitemen who stumbled across our world had no experience in how we thought and believed. They couldn't grasp the concept of peoples living with the sun and moon. Peoples whose time was not measured by hourglasses or clocks, but by what was happening on the earth and in the sky. Peoples who looked at animals to judge when a season was passing and changing. Peoples who acted together, in consensus, because to do otherwise was unspeakable and foolish. Peoples who were not ashamed or afraid of bodily functions or sexual acts. Peoples who had a rhythm that pulsed to that of Earth. The whiteman saw none of this except for the unashamed celebration of sexuality. They were so spellbound, they filled reams of paper on the subject. The Jesuits especially gloried in recounting every sexual act. The Spanish and French wrote home to Europe about the sexual "looseness" of Native women. Of course, these men did not mention the word rape, a common occurrence perpetrated on my women ancestors. Nor did they write back home about our spirituality, except to call us heathens. Neither explorer nor the religious saw our physical presence in *our* own context, nor heard the prayers that were a joyous song to being part of the natural. To this day, the whiteman continues to look at Indigenous Peoples from *their* context, fitting us into *their* limited and limiting view of Earth.

Church and state have long worked as consorts in the colonization of Aboriginal peoples. With the guns came the Bible. With the Bible came the whiskey. With the whiskey came addiction and government over our affairs. With government came reserves, and loathing of all that was natural. With loathing came the unnatural; the internalization of all they told us about ourselves. And the beliefs hold fast in some. There are christian Indians, and there are homophobic Indians. In speaking with an Elder from Tyendinaga, I asked her how things had changed in her ninety-six years of life. She started to cry and said, "We learned all sorts of bad things from the whites. Now we no longer lover each other." And perhaps this is the key to understanding homophobia within my Nation. The love that was natural in our world, has become unnatural as we become more consumed by the white world and the values therein. Our sexuality has been colonized, sterilized, whitewashed. Our sense of spirit has been sterilized, colonized, made over to pander to a growing consumer need for quick and easy redemption. What the dominant culture has never been able to comprehend is that spirit/sex/prayer/flesh/religion/natural is who I am as a Two-Spirit. "Now we no longer love each other." What a triumph for the whiteman and the cultural enslavement he brought to the First Nations. When we fight amongst ourselves as to who is a better Indian, who is a more traditional Indian, we are linking arms with the ones who would just as soon see us dead. Homophobia has *no* justification within our Nations.

My partner and I have a small cottage on Walpole Island in Ontario. Walpole Island is held by a confederacy known as the Council of Three Fires—Potawatomi, Ottawa, Ojibwa, and since it comprises several islands, there are numerous canals and tiny channels of water where only a canoe can get through. Denise and I canoe every chance we get. We both love the steady movement of paddles in the water, the sounds of marsh birds, the glimpse of turtles under the water, the sun on our faces, that wondrous smell of fertility all around us, and sometimes the special gift of finding a feather or a nest floating by us. On this one day, we found a small patch of dry land with a black willow growing straight out of the earth. There was a noisy Red-wing flying in and out of the branches. We hesitated before beaching the canoe, knowing how protective these birds are, and not wanting to disturb him or the nest he might be guarding. But he flew away and we climbed out onto the land. We talked, ate our lunch, breathed the air, then lay under the willow and touched each other, kissed, made love between us. As I felt the first tremors of orgasm take hold of me, a Blue Heron entered my body and I became her. Each pulse of orgasm was a flap of wings, a preparation for flight, and as orgasm took hold of me, I felt myself lifting from the ground, wings gathering strength, flying. I opened my long, yellow beak and gave a cry. Later, I asked Denise if she had heard the voice of Heron. "No dearest, I only heard yours."

In this moment of time and place, Heron had chosen me to communicate her cries of freedom, power and joy in being the magnificent creature she is. She told me that her joy was mine and mine was hers. This is a physical prayer. This is creation. This is what cannot be stolen from me, or frightened out of me. Although Heron has not come to me again in that special intimate way, when

I see her flying, or standing still in water, the long curve of her neck sparkling and shimmering in the sunlight, I feel, once again, the wonder of the great mysteries that are part of the natural order of my worlds.

Those people who despise sex also despise Heron and others like her. The need to "have dominion over the earth" is not a natural or healthy way to be on Earth. There have been numerous books and articles written by white feminists to describe the hatred of women that is carried over to nature. If men can't kill all women, they will attempt to kill all that lives, especially that which comes from Mother Earth. While I agree with some of this theorizing, I feel it does not encompass Aboriginal thought, or any theories about lesbianism. There is also no mention of enchantment, or to use a better word, *orenda*, a Mohawk description of what cannot be explained but is accepted as the natural order of life. Perhaps even in feminism it is too difficult to give up a belief in the Eurocentric way of living and being.

A Native man may be sexist, but lovingly tend corn and beans, say a prayer of forgiveness for killing a deer or moose for his family, and believe fully in the power of magic in his life. I am reminded of a gathering of Native writers that took place in 1992. A Mohawk man gave a speech in which he exhibited the worst kinds of white-leftist haranguing. Some of the women in the audience were angry at his patronizing behavior and obvious sexism. It was discussed who would speak to him. *I* was selected—because I am Mohawk, because I am his elder by ten or fifteen years. I did speak to him. He listened, albeit, angrily at first. And I knew that this was a man who cared passionately about the environment, about children, who spoke the language of our ancestors, but nevertheless had internalized the European/Marxist thought of male domination, and the macho posturing that comes with it. Sexism is a learned behaviour, not a natural behaviour in Aboriginal cultures. And one can call himself traditional and still be sexist.

The Longhouse religion of recent use comes from the Code of Handsome Lake, or *Gai'wiio'*. Handsome Lake, Seneca Nation, was a reformed alcoholic who had many dreams of a new religion. Born in 1735, in his later years he was terribly aggrieved at the havoc brought to his people by the whiteman. While a man who cared deeply and strongly about his people, Handsome Lake introduced many christian-based concepts and "ways" that he exhorted the People to follow. Among those messages were "marriage" between men and women, the christian concept of adultery and the "forgiveness" of it (if committed by a husband), the disbanding of animal societies and the dances to honour these Totems, the ban against homosexuality, the confessing of witchcraft and the cessation of such practice, the ban on women employing herbs and medicines for the purpose of abortion or birth control. It is interesting to me that witchcraft, as seen by Handsome Lake, was a female activity that involved the seduction of men to perform ugly acts, but the practice of curing and healing was a male activity, thus these practitioners were known as Medicine Men. I find this curiously christian and antithetical to old Iroquois belief, where women held the knowledge of healing and the mysteries of Earth and cosmos.

Before his death in 1815, Handsome Lake carried his message to the People of the Iroquois Confederacy and it has held firm among many of the People. I find nothing traditionally Onkwehonwe in this religion. Homophobia can thrive in the uneasy mixture of christian thought and Aboriginal belief. And it does. If sexism is a learned behavior, so also is homophobia. They can be unlearned, if the desire is present. Some of the unlearning has to begin with us, the Two-Spirits.

Much of the self-hatred we carry around inside us is centuries old. This self-hatred is so coiled within itself, we often cannot distinguish the racism from the homophobia from the sexism. We carry the stories of our grandmothers, our ancestors. And some of these stories are ugly and terrorizing. And some are beautiful testaments to endurance and dignity. We must learn to emulate this kind of testimony. Speaking ourselves out loud—for our people, for ourselves. To deny our sexuality is to deny our part in creation.

The denial of sexuality and of those who live according to their sexuality is almost unspeakable. It has been named homophobia, but that bland word does not tell of the blasphemous acts committed against us in the name of religion and state. I use the word because that is what it is—a defilement of all that is spirit-filled and ceremonial. I also believe that the hatred and violence that is directed against us is a result of the hatred against their god. It must be difficult to follow doctrine that orders them to live perfect, sex-empty, anti-sensual lives, then turn around and behold *us*, the perverts that god also made. This must drive the christians insane with anger. We get away with it and are not punished by this god that exhorts *them* to be good or else! Of course, the more fundamentalist types say AIDS is a punishment. But even this theology is falling by the wayside as more and more heterosexuals and children are being infected. If one hates the god who made them, they can turn that hatred inward and outward to people who are not like them. I have often thought that racism, sexism, homophobia are results of a giant cultural and religious inferiority psychosis. I realize this is not an original theory, but I adhere to the basic premise of it.

Those of us who are Two-Spirit do not believe we are better, smarter, more spiritual or more *Indian* than others. We do not proselytize, promise salvation and redemption, sell amulets or holy cards to a heaven. We do not promise a better life by saving heterosexual souls. We do not tell stories of men dying on crosses to incite guilt. We do live our lives in the best way we can. We do attempt to appreciate the unique position we have in our communities. We are not "just like everybody else." That line is for those who are still trying to prove themselves worthy of the dominant culture's approval.

I think the 1993 March on Washington for "Lesbians, Gay, and Bi Equal Rights and Liberating" made many mistakes in trying to look and act "just like everybody else." One of the more endearing and daring facets of being gay/lesbian/bi is the outlandishness that permeates our communities. What's wrong with being different from the asexual and conservative culture that actually makes laws about sex and who we do it with?! Why would we want to be accepted by them? Why would we want to be like them? Why the emphasis on the military? Is our main concern that of serving in armies that routinely invade countries that have large populations of people of colour? Is this the agenda we want to be associated with?

During the 1994 celebration and march honouring the twenty-fifth anniversary of the Stonewall riots and the beginning of the gay liberation movement, gay-punks carried signs: stonewall was a riot, not a name brand and your pride = their profits. Instead of turning our gatherings into photo-ops and mainstream-acceptable, capitalist enterprises, we need to *celebrate* our outlaw status in the dominant society and embrace our differences. I'm with the gay-punks. I will not prove myself to anyone. I am a mother—a lesbian mother. I am a grandmother—a lesbian grandmother. I am the lesbian daughter of my mother and father. I am the lesbian lover of women. I am the lesbian partner of Denise. I am the lesbian being who welcomes Heron, Turtle and Moose into my life. I am the lesbian being who prays with words, heart and body. I am a Two-Spirit woman of the Mohawk Nation. I am a lesbian who listens to the spirits who guide me. I am a Two-Spirit who walks this path my ancestors cleared for us. I will not go away; in fact, I will be in-you-face as long as I breathe the air of this life. If I can clear more brush and cut through thickets, I will. For I feel that we also make tradition in our various and various communities and Nations. This tradition is generous and welcoming. It is a tradition of wholeness and honour. It is a tradition of remembrance and fidelity.

Writing as Witness[1]

Why are the words "Native" and "vision" used together so often? I expect it comes from the place that wishes to ghettoize and confirm our "quaintness" for the dominant culture.

There is a spiritual practice that occurs in many First Nations peoples of venturing out alone to an isolated place to experience a dream, an interaction with spirits, a communion with animal beings *in order to find a life-time path to dwell on.* This practice has been translated into the English language as a "vision quest." Like many Aboriginal words that have been interpreted by the Europeans, "vision quest" hardly begins to explain a complicated religious ceremony that is one of seeking balance and centredness. I suspect that white people consider this "quest" an everyday occurrence for Native peoples because it confirms their view of Natives as "exotic" and more "spiritual" than non-Natives. Like many spiritual practices of First Nations peoples, the idea of vision questing has been "borrowed" by the dominant culture for use in superficial ritual that usually costs money. And the word "vision" is pasted onto anything that concerns Native peoples, as if we are the spiritual nannies of dominant society. It also serves as a way to keep us invisible, except for the occasions when we are trotted out for exhibition as the mood suits the dominant culture. My cultural definition of vision is a vast and far-reaching one. It is also a holy one. I doubt if I have more vision or spirituality than an Irish woman, a Polish woman, an African-American woman. I am a Mohawk woman and my dreams, my beliefs, my vision are why I am on the writing path.

In many of my stories there are moments when the protagonist is faced with two choices—to live or to die. Often these choices are brought about because of a circumstance involving the death

---

1 From a panel entitled "Native American Vision," given at Michigan State University, June 1991.

of a loved one. And this moment of reckoning is brought to the protagonist by a being that is not human. This reckoning is also a reclamation.

Since contact with white people, our battle for survival has not left us free of the internalization of European and christian values. Where death was once viewed as a necessary and natural piece of life's cycle, we often find ourselves in the unnatural state of thinking that death is something to fear or something that we would be better off achieving. "Better dead than Red."

During these five hundred years, the shattering of our cultural and community systems has often led to a split within our individual selves and souls. We want to "forget" all that is Indian, because the remembering is so painful and heartbreaking. This has led to a kind of spiritual malaise or limbo. The erosion of self that accompanies that malaise is another curse of colonialism. We have seen that curse at work in our communities—alcoholism, drug addiction, disrespect for women, incest, suicide, homophobia; these evils are the result of the self-loathing that imperialism has forced into our minds. This is the rape that has left a legacy of unnatural acts in its wake. We are living the testament of that rape every day in our heads. There are times when I am awestruck by the fact that we, as Aboriginal peoples, are still managing to direct our lives and those of our children and grandchildren.

In my story, "Swimming Upstream," the protagonist, Anna May, has come to the reckoning of her life. She has lost her son in a drowning, not through any fault she has committed, but she sees the death of her son as a grievous mistake in a long line of mistakes brought about by her very existence. As a Native woman, a half-breed, a Two-Spirit, she has believed the message of that long-ago *and* present imperative—she deserves to die for the "sins" of being who she is. Anna May chooses to run away from her loving relationship with Catherine, chooses to buy a bottle of wine, "the red, sweet kind that will make her forget," chooses the death that is most familiar to her—alcoholism. What Anna May does not realize, and what I did not realize until *after* I wrote the story, is that Anna May was not acting upon a choice, she was reacting to the encoded rape of her mind by colonization. She was doing what she was supposed to do as a Native—turn death into an ignominious statement, rather than a part of the natural continuum. Anna May was imbalanced, the madness manifested in First Nations people as a result of colonialism.

As I was writing the story, I began to be carried along with Anna May's journey. Instead of directing the events, some other presence started to direct me. I remembered vividly the Bruce Peninsula and the Sauble Falls that contained the hundreds of Salmon who were swimming upstream to spawn. At this point, on the page, Anna May drove her car to that very place I had seen, her bottle of wine unopened in the car. She stopped her car, got out, saw the Salmon, saw the painful, yet beautiful struggle to carry life to new beginnings and new generations. I believe that Salmon was guiding my fingers on the keys. Just as he guided his body and his regeneration into new waters, I was writing with the sounds of water, the sounds of Salmon jumping and flying to get to their mates, to *renew* life, to renew *life*.

As an Indigenous writer, I feel that the gift of writing and the *privilege* of writing holds a responsibility to be a witness to my people. To be a witness of the natural world, to be a witness to Salmon, to Anna May, to her son, to the sometimes unbearable circumstances of our lives. Anna May's "choice" to relive the pain that would lead to death—alcohol—was stopped by the power and magic of Salmon. Her vision of death is turned upon itself. She is directed by the natural, the Indigenous, the real. She sees her son in the water, swimming to another way of being, another place, a place she cannot enter with dishonour. Thus, Anna May makes a real choice. She turns her car around and proceeds back home. She will begin the slow process of healing her mind. She will throw away the old messages, the old codes. She will make new ones, for herself, for her people. At least, this is what I think, for by now, Anna May is not just a protagonist in a story, she is a real being in my life. Salmon has not only given me his story, he has given me hers. And when I read this story aloud to groups of people, so many come to me after and tell me that this is their story also. And so many Native people speak to me of their renewal, their choice to be a witness to our history.

In another story, "This Place," David, a young gay Native, returns to his Reserve to die. He has lived in the city for much of his adult life, and comes home because he has AIDS and wants to be among his people and on his land for the act of death. Yet David fears death. He is terrorized by what he does not know, or rather, what he does not "remember." David left the Reserve feeling he did not belong because of his homosexuality. And while he has not given up his Nativehood in the city, he has put parts of himself aside in order to survive. David has large amounts of anger towards his people for the homophobia he perceives, and large amounts of anger towards the white, gay, male community he knows to be racist. His mother calls in a medicine man, Joseph, to help David reconcile his life *and* death. Joseph brings many things with him, a piece of mirror, a feather from a Whistling Swan, a document written by David's ancestor, a snake skin, and a cat. This cat, The Prophet, named after the great Shawnee warrior, is the means through which David sees death as one of the many parts of the whole. Joseph, who is also gay, takes David on many journeys, gathering up the pieces that David lost or cast aside in his struggle to be a gay Native man in a white world that despises both. The homophobia that David perceives in his people is not imagined. As First Nations people, our spiritual loss includes the dishonouring of our gay and lesbian citizens. This painful rebuff leads many of us to leave our ancestral lands to look for support elsewhere. For many of us, this meant large cities, seeking others who shared a like sexuality, perhaps even finding a kind of anonymity. We were anathematized, or at least, made to feel like we were a curse to our own people. David was also imbalanced. Like Anna May, the effects of colonial domination had seeped into his mind, his heart. Thus, his fear of facing death, a fear he "knew" was required of him.

I am also a respectful admirer of Cat. I do not think she is "cute" nor do I think of her as a pet. She is distinguished and elegant. Brilliant and knowing. Wise and very, very old. Her insistence and persistence (I am only human and it takes me longer to "get it") brought much of this story to fruition. It is no coincidence that my beloved Maggie sat in my room during the writing of this story, grooming herself, watching me with her green eyes, occasionally walking across my keyboard to keep me in line.

While writing this story, I thought about many of the Native gay men I have met. Some are in the Spirit World, some are living with AIDS on Reserves and in cities. Some are HIV negative, some have just been diagnosed. All are courageous and lovely. David is all of them, and he is also the Native man who fears the natural process of death. Some of us are not fortunate enough to have a holy person, a shaman to guide our feelings and spirits through the many labyrinths and mysteries we call death. The great act of remembering *who we are* can bring acceptance of the Mystery.

What I want to say is this. Vision is not just a perception of what is possible, it is a window to the perception of what is possible, it is a window to the knowledge of what *has* happened and what *is* happening. Our side of the window shows some unlovely and frightening acts that, for us, the Indigenous peoples of this continent, continue to be re-enacted. But there is a crack in the window that allows us the real view, the natural state of being. It is through this crack that our writers slip the stories, the words, sending them out to be ignored, burned, or found and cherished, carried along by the wind, by a bird, by a woman who retells the stories to her young. This is our tradition. Our words *are* the vision, given with generosity and hope. There is nothing "quaint" in this.

From E. Pauline Johnson to Nicole Tanguay, our words and stories have undergone numerous transfigurations. What we once *told* is now being *written.* The legacy of our community rape is being transformed into a new legacy of hope, truth and self-love. I feel my own work has changed and renewed itself: has lived, has died, has lived—will die again, will live again. There was a time when I believed and even said out loud that I was not a writer any longer. I was in thrall to self-loathing, to the false legacy, to the unnatural. It is no coincidence that during that time I didn't hear the birds' singing, I didn't see the seeds making themselves over into corn, I didn't feel the love that was being sent to me. I had ceased to think Mohawk. I was a victim of the message. Though I managed to crawl, to dog-paddle out of that abyss, it would not have been possible if the natural world had not insisted itself upon me. I was overwhelmed with sensations of higher beings. I saw a Yellow-Headed Blackbird, stopping in the Midwest before continuing on to the West. Blue Herons appeared everywhere. I smelled grass. I heard corn growing. I felt love and its effect on my body through orgasm. I became Mohawk again. I became me again.

The abundance of Earth's messages drowned out the un-Earthly message. Story gave itself to me. I began to write again.

We have been forced to reject and thereby forget what has made us real as Native peoples. The dominant society longs for this forgetfulness on our part. It hungers for our assimilation into their world, their beliefs, their code. And it hurries this process along by promises of acceptance and forgiveness. Their paranoia threatens to become our own. But what we may have "forgotten" is still in our blood. Salmon's desire to go home is our desire also. Blue Heron's desire to fly long distances to make a home is ours also. Corn's desire to grow is ours also. For we are parts of them and they are parts of us. This is why we are Indigenous. This is what none of us *has* truly forgotten, though the false message pounds and thrashes our minds. Who we are is written on our bodies, our hearts, our souls. This is what it means to be Native in the dawn of the twenty-first century. Witness to what has been and what is to be. Knowing what has transpired and dreaming of what will come. Listening to the stories brought to us by other beings. Renewing ourselves in the midst of chaos.

May Salmon's story always be carried in our blood. May David's story be remembered with honour. This is my vision and hope. This is why I write.

Afterword: Beth Brant's Gift

Beth Brant helped save my life. I never met Beth Brant.
Both of these things are true.

"A Long Story" begins with a dedication to both of Beth Brant's great-great grandmothers, followed by two epigraphs—one from an 1892 newspaper, noting the departure of "about 40 Indian children. . . for the Philadelphia Indian School," and the second from a book titled *Legal Kidnapping* by Anna Demeter, stating "I am only beginning to understand what it means for a mother to lose a child." Even before this story begins, Brant documents the separation of mothers and children by the patriarchal whims of white men and their laws, speaks the grief that women are warned not to speak, that courts do not want to hear, that the media will not cover. Even before the story begins, Beth tells women like me one important thing: *you are not alone.*

Beth Brant crafts alternating vignettes that follow an Indigenous woman named Annie in 1890-91, and a woman named Mary in 1978-79, through journeys of grief after their children have been taken from them—Annie, because the colonizing white government feels it knows what is best for Indian children; Mary, because the patriarchal white government feels it knows what is best for the child of a lesbian. Mary is never spoken of as Indigenous, but Brant makes it clear that the two characters are related in sisterhood through their shared loss; Annie and Mary mirror each other's grief as women and mothers across time and space.

In the aftermath of her two young children taken to a government boarding school far away, Annie can't eat, ignores her body's needs, isolates herself from her community. She has visions of the future for herself and her husband, her children, and her Indigenous community: a river of blood coming to drown everything. She tears up a letter from her children and buries the pieces in the earth, knowing that the boarding school teachers control its contents. She refuses to acknowledge that the "Martha" and "Daniel" who sign the letter are her children, and in very real ways, Annie is right: they are no longer the children named She Sees the Deer and He Catches Leaves that were taken away.

What Brant makes clear in this story is Annie's refusal to silence her grief: she howls through the night, cuts off her hair and burns it, cuts her arms, makes her grief both visible and audible. She does this all publicly, not in private, not alone. She demands that her grief be heard. As a result, she becomes known as "the crazy woman." Still, Annie refuses to remain silent about the criminal violence she and her family experience. These expressions of grief and rage are all Annie has left with which to resist. She grieves the ways her children's Indigenous identities are erased, and how she, as their mother, is erased from their lives.

In the 1979 thread, Mary knows that "it's the word *lesbian* that makes them panic, that makes them afraid, makes them destroy children." Her ex-husband has fought for and been granted custody of six-year-old Patricia based on Mary's sexual orientation. 1979 is only six years after the American Psychiatric Association (APA) asked members whether homosexuality was an actual mental disorder. Because the vote was almost evenly divided, the APA compromised, removing homosexuality from the Diagnostic Statistical Manual, but replacing it with 'sexual orientation disturbance' for people 'in conflict with' their sexual orientation." The truth is, not until 1987 did the APA completely dismiss homosexuality as a form of mental illness and real change lagged far behind.[1] Beth Brant is painfully aware of these slippages.

Like Annie, Mary receives a letter from her daughter, one she knows Patricia's father stood over and dictated to her. The letter erases Ellen, Patricia's other mother, from her life entirely, nearly erases Mary, and denies Patricia a real voice of her own. Like Annie, Mary destroys this letter, seeing it as the voice of her ex-husband and lawyers, not her daughter's. Like Annie, one hundred and twelve years before her, Mary also has flashes of a future devastation: "He will teach her to hate us. He will!"

---

1   As we know, even now we still fight for acknowledgment of this basic human right.

Although Mary's lover, Ellen, offers to leave "if it will make it better," Mary does not even consider this possibility. Instead, she turns to Ellen and they comfort one another in tender lovemaking that celebrates life; Mary says, "I shout, I sing, I weep salty liquid, sweet and warm it coats her throat..." Mary's vocalizations and affirmations of love praise the ways that the couple's lovemaking creates and honors life. Mary's voice emerges as a declaration of finding joy in life even without her child. This doesn't mean that Mary chooses Ellen over Patricia; it means that life is that sacred, that much of a gift.

Mary's story ends in 1979, when Mary finally accepts the fact that her daughter will never be allowed to return. In a powerful scene, Mary rages at the patriarchal powers who have "won" Patricia for her father; she tears apart her daughter's room, and "a noise gathers in my throat and finds the way out. I begin a scream that turns to howling, then becomes hoarse choking." At first, that scream feels like nothing but pure anguish. But as the scene continues, we hear that scream against the history of Mary's previous, obedient silence. Now, with her unsanctioned voice, Mary owns her reality: "Lesbian. *I am one.* Even for Patricia, even for her, *I will not cease to be!*" Kneeling in the scraps of curtains, sheets and blankets, Mary realizes that "all the judges in their flapping robes, and the fathers who look for revenge, are ground, ground into dust and disappear with the wind." And in that moment of destruction, Mary feels "the blood pumping outward to my veins, carrying nourishment and life." She walks out of the room, shuts the door behind her; she walks back into her life as a woman who will not be destroyed. Transformed, yes—but not destroyed.

But Brant isn't done with this "long story." In 1891, Annie's entire world is collapsing. She has nightmares or visions of the decimation of her people, of the earth soaking up their blood and "becoming a thing there is no name for." If naming is a powerful act, a thing so horrible it cannot be named is still more frightening. Annie's final, heartbreaking words in "A Long Story" are, "A crazy woman. That is what they call me." She doesn't deny it. She says it with weariness, resignation, even—like Mary—a kind of acceptance.

If insanity is the only honest response to what has happened to her, then Annie is crazy. If insanity is a badge of honor awarded to one who sees the truth of colonization and kidnapping and murder, and calls it out, then yes, Annie is crazy. *She speaks the truth.* She refuses to self-medicate, accommodate, assimilate, or ignore the brutality she experiences. She witnesses to the love she feels for her children, her people, her homeland, even if to witness means pain. For Annie to remain that committed, that true, that constant, in the face of an oppressor who tries to silence her at every turn, is to hold ground in a way that is almost inexpressibly courageous.

For many years, I let Annie bear my suffering. I am not able, yet, to claim my own.

1994. I am a young mixed-blood mother of two, married to a much older white man, struggling to reconcile my indigenous identity, my romantic and sexual attraction to other women, and my daily life. I have a very short list of Native lesbian writers to whose work I can turn for emotional and psychic sustenance: Chrystos (Menominee), Janice Gould (Koyangk'auwi Maidu), Vickie Sears (Cherokee) and Beth Brant (Mohawk). Published Indigenous lesbian writers are few and far between in the early 1990s, and "published" means that small presses often run on a wing and a prayer, available in limited quantities to limited geographic areas. Each of these writers has significant impact on my ability to survive the conflagrations in my life, but only Beth Brant can speak to me as one mother to another. In particular, "A Long Story" wraps itself around me like wise arms, and hangs on.

In 1995, I confess to my husband that I am in love with another woman; the first words out of his mouth are the only words in the world that could keep me from leaving him: "You'll never see those kids again."

A shock runs through my body like a whip. Something old and wordless opens inside me. "You would really prefer to have me live here, like *this*—against my will—you would really take away the kids?" I finally ask, from the edge of that chasm.

"Yes." he says. "I would. I'll find a lawyer who'll do it. It won't be hard."

I believe him. In the blink of an eye, I'm in the belly of the beast: fear.

In the days and months that follow, I have no name for the terror I feel, no explanation for my inability to eat or keep food down, the swift loss of 40 pounds, a sudden thyroid problem that makes my hair fall out, gives my heart palpitations, leaves my skin grey and dry. All I know is that my children are being held hostage, and only my "good behavior" can save them. I must be a "good mother." Bad mothers lose their babies.

My own mother lost three of her children: one, a death due to neglect; two others to foster care. The youngest—me—not lost, exactly, but caught in a brutal cycle of abandonment and tenuous reclamation.

Annie's tears and Mary's voice honor everything I cannot speak: the loss of my lover, fear of being unmasked as a lesbian and having my children taken away. Unlike Annie, my grief cannot be spoken out loud. I cry only when alone; public sadness would be an admission of guilt. Like Mary, I wait for a moment of clarity.

It isn't a pretty time. I do what I have to do. I fall back on survival skills from my childhood. I become a tiny, tiny silent soul inside a body more like a robot than a human being. I lie. I pretend I am "recovering" from the love I could not have. I celebrate holidays, give birthday parties, volunteer at my children's elementary school. I write coded poems about grief and desire.

Inside the heating vent of the little back room I use as an office, I hide Beth Brant's books, but carry her stories—filled with protections against depression and despair—inside the small leather pouch that is my heart.

No, I never met Beth Brant. But I hung onto her stories even as my life frayed like a rope bearing too much weight.

Beth Brant's stories were the strands that strengthened my own torn fibers.

Crawling out of my fear—slowly, clumsily—I won acceptance to grad school, applied for loans, earned a teaching assistantship to help pay my way, studied Native American women's poetry. I began attending conferences and readings where I met other Native scholars and authors. But Beth Brant and I were never in the same place at the same time. I finally left my marriage just before my dissertation year (children old enough to assert their own agency in dividing their time between two households), but I was still closeted, afraid to start a new relationship. I needed an actual home rather than a tiny apartment above a meth lab. I needed a paycheck, health insurance and a car. I needed to no longer fear that the wrong whisper or comment about my sexual orientation would bring about an apocalypse.

What I had: two fiercely loving children. An accepting mother of my own. The assistance of many angels, friends, helpers who came to me in dreams or as living, generous souls. I had Margo, the dear friend who would later become my wife.

I had Beth Brant's stories. I kept her books on a corner of my desk, a little altar of faith, as I wrote a dissertation about Native American women's love poetry and erotics.

When I graduated with a Ph.D. and a tenure-track job in 2001, my mother, my children Miranda and Danny, and Margo, sat in the audience at the University of Washington, and cheered when my name was called. Physically exhausted and deeply in debt, I didn't know yet that my mother had only six months left to live. I didn't know yet how difficult guiding two children through adolescence would be, or how the first three years of a tenure-track job would test me, or how the trauma in my childhood would continue to hold me back in forming and healing relationships.

But I did know that this was *my life*. At last.

Beth Brant's books came with me through every move, ending up on a shelf with other Native-authored books in a university built with enslaved labor, on Indigenous land. That shelf of books is closest to my desk, like a shield for my heart.

One evening in August of 2015, a friend wrote to tell me that Beth Brant had walked on. My wife and I sat down at the table; I told Margo about Beth's stories, the ones that walked me through and out the other side of suicide. Margo knows this terrain; she was my friend then, though living far away at the time. Still, on that day, she listened as my wife, and held my hand. "We owe Beth Brant a lot," she said to me. I felt those words find a home in my chest. Yes. I owed Beth so much. And I never told her.

I walked upstairs to my desk, wrote a blog post from my heart. Tried to say what it was that Beth's work did, and still does, in the world. A few weeks later, Julie Enszer of Sinister Wisdom wrote to say she had read my blog post, asked if I'd like to be part of *Sinister*

Wisdom's Sapphic Classic series that she envisioned as a collection of Beth Brant's stories and essays. I hesitated, not sure that I was the right person to do that. After all, I didn't know Beth.

But her stories tell me that she knew I was out there.

I told Julie yes.

In her essays, Beth writes that she experiences her writing as a gift, received from the spirits in the form of Eagle, who stopped her in her tracks and communicated with her "a message." The details of that message, she elaborates, tell her that "the gift of writing and the *privilege* of writing holds a responsibility to be a witness to my people. To be a witness of the natural world..." and to "use this gift on behalf of love." Beth reminds us that to share this gift is essential; "giving, receiving, giving—it makes a complete circle of Indigenous truth." Beth Brant leaves much knowledge and love behind, and I am grateful that Sinister Wisdom has the foresight to collect, honor, and make her writings available to the ones Beth knew would be out there, are still out there, those who are still to come.

Beth's words gave me—still give me—the courage to face my own encounters with beings much like Salmon or Eagle: powerful beings whose knowledge of the larger cycles and spirals of existence teach us about our responsibilities, bestow the skills and strength we need to live meaningful Indigenous lives. Her words show me that a path towards reclaiming a whole self is possible, that the pain of transformation is part of that path. The choice is not to be happy or unhappy, to fail or succeed; the choice is to *live*. To take the losses and abandonments, push on through them to the life that still awaits. To honor Creation by accepting these gifts.

Nimasianexelpasaleki: thank you, Beth Brant. May your memory be a blessing. We never said *hello,* so why say *goodbye*? Micha ene hikpalala—I'll see you.

Deborah A. Miranda
September 20, 2018
Lexington, Virginia

BIBLIOGRAPHY

Books:
Food & Spirits. Ithaca, NY: Firebrand Books, 1991.

A Gathering of Spirit: A Collection by North American Women. Editor. Amherst, MA: Sinister Wisdom 22/23, 1983. Ithaca, NY: Firebrand Books, 1988. Toronto: The Women›s Press, 1988.

I'll Sing' til the Day I Die: Conversations with Tyendinaga Elders. Toronto: McGilligan Books, 1995.

Mohawk Trail. Ithaca, NY: Firebrand Books, 1985.

In a Vast Dreaming. Toronto: Native Women in the Arts, 1995.

Writing as Witness: Essay and Talk. Toronto: Women's Press, 1994.

Anthologies in Which Brant Appears:
Bruchac, Joseph, ed. *Songs from This Earth on Turtle's Back: Contemporary American Indian Poetry.* Greenfield Center, NY: Greenfield Review Press, 1983.

Dykewords: An Anthology of Lesbian Writing. Ed. Lesbian Writing and Publishing Collective. Toronto: Women's Press, 1990.

Piercy, Marge, ed. *Early Ripening: Poetry by Women.* New York, Pandora Books, 1987.

Roscoe, Will, ed. *Living the Spirit: A Gay American Indian Anthology.* New York: St. Martin's Press, 1988.

Other Works:
"Grandmothers of a New World." *Women of Power* 16 (Spring 1990): 40-47.

"Giveaway: Native Lesbian Writers." *Signs: Journal of Women in Culture and Society* 18 (Summer 1993): 944-947.

"The Good Red Road." *American Indian Culture and Research Journal* 21.1 (1997): 193-206.

Critical Work about Brant:

Cullum, Linda E. *Contemporary American Ethnic Poets: Lives, Works, Sources* . Greenwood Publishing Group, 2004.

Day, Frances A. *Lesbian and Gay Voices: An Annotated Bibliography and Guide to Literature for Children and Young Adults.* Greenwood Publishing Group, 2000.

Kostić, Milena and Vesna Lopičić. "'I will not cease to be': voicing the alternative in Beth Brant's 'A Long Story.'" *The Central European Journal of Canadian Studies* 8.1 (2002): 23-30.

Sonneborn, Liz. *A to Z of American Indian Women.* Infobase Publishing, 2014.

Byron, Glennis and Andrew J. Sneddon. *The Body and the Book: Writings on Poetry and Sexuality.* Rodopi, 2008.

Womack, Craig S. *Art as Performance, Story as Criticism.* University of Oklahoma Press, 2014.

Reviews of Brant's Work:

Danielson, Linda L. "*Reviewed Work: Mohawk Trail.*" *Studies in American Indian Literatures* Series 2, 5.1 (1993): 103- 107.

Jakoski, Helen. "Beth Brant (Degonwadonti). *Mohawk Trail .*" *Explorations of Sights and Sounds Journal* 9 (Summer 1989): 9-10. Web.

Johnson, Lisa N. "A Review of *Food and Spirits.*" glbtrt.ala.org, GLBT Reviews from ALA's Gay Lesbian Bisexual Transgender Round Table. 1991. Web.

Justice, Daniel Heath. "Daniel Heath Justice recommends *Writing as Witness* by Beth Brant." Edited by Jane van Koeverden. CBC.ca (Canadian Broadcasting Corporation), CBC Books, 2017. Web.

Biography:

"Beth Brant" under *Poets*, Poetry Foundation, https://www.poetryfoundation.org/poets/beth-brant

Janice Gould was of mixed European and Concow (koyangk'auwi) descent and grew up in Berkeley, California. She was a graduate of the University of California at Berkeley, where she received degrees in Linguistics and English, and of the University of New Mexico, where she earned her Ph.D. in English. She recently earned a Master's degree in Library Science from the University of Arizona. Janice's books of poetry include *Beneath My Heart* (1990), *Earthquake Weather* (1996), *Alphabet* (an art book/chapbook, 1990), *Doubters and Dreamers* (2011), *The Force of Gratitude* (2017), and *Seed* (2019). She was the co-editor of *Speak to Me Words: Essays on American Indian Poetry* (2003), published by the University of Arizona. Janice was an associate professor in Women's and Ethnic Studies at the University of Colorado, Colorado Springs, where she developed and directed the concentration in Native American Studies. Janice died on June 28, 2019 after a battle with pancreatic cancer.